The Last Train Home

TONY WILSON

THE LAST TRAIN HOME

FIRST EDITION

Published by Lulu.com

ISBN: 978-1-291-11242-9

If you enjoyed this book please consider posting a
review for it as every mention helps. Many thanks.

FOR DAD

Who was the first to instill the magic.
Time has not dimmed our memory or our love.

ACKNOWLEDGEMENTS:

First and foremost, thanks to my mum and dad for making our childhood Christmases so special that they lived long in to adulthood and inspired me to write the book in the first place. Thanks also to all those I pestered to read it and for their words of encouragement and advice, including Tim Bryan, Esther Bryan, Abi Mortimer, Cath O'Hanlan and Leila Bahaijoub. To Dan King, who helped me format the book and let me inveigle myself on to his quiz team with spectacular results, for which he still resents me. For Charles Dickens for writing the only real Christmas book that matters. And finally, thanks and all my love to my wonderful family, Lucy, JJ, Amy and Holly, who bring me such joy, despite the mess and tidying up.

PROLOGUE:
THE BEGINNING

The hour was late and night had long ago fallen with the abruptness of winter, yet darkness had still to spread across the parched and ancient land. Such was the light with which it shone. Its rays had no warmth, they had travelled too far, but they bathed the desert in a silver hue so bright it was as if the night air had lost its ability to chill.

Its presence had not gone unnoticed. Night time creatures, programmed to expect the oily darkness of a new moon, scampered across the sand and disappeared down their burrows, agitated and hungry; camels refused to sleep and became restless, their guttural braying carrying for miles in the stillness; bedouins blew their horns to alert other tribes across the dunes; goat herders gathered their livestock together and slept amongst them looking up at the sky; and everyone built their fires higher and slept closer than normal. The desert air chattered with a mixture of fear and expectation.

Out in the huge, featureless plain that spread between the jagged hills and the shifting dunes sat a man, solitary and thoughtful, staring in to the night. He dug his hand in to the fine sand and watched as the grains tumbled through his fingers. How strange to be alone, he thought. No servants, no ladies-in-waiting, no trumpeters, no fools. He did not miss them. The paraphernalia of court, once so colourful and exciting, had grown tiresome over the years and the daily pressure of an entire kingdom seeking imperial guidance now ground and exhausted him. The thrill of power fades most rapidly in those born to high office, he reflected.

It was the first time he had really been alone. He could remember several times as a child sitting on his bed, crying, feeling by himself in the world, but that was different. Even at such at young age he was aware that he only had to ask and he would be brought someone to play with, something to interest and amuse him. But now...

He had left the royal caravan at the mountain pass shortly after dawn and at his insistence had continued on through the desert alone with his camel, much to the despair of his advisers and to the surprise of himself. Why he had acted so was beyond him. He had never craved solitude; he had, in fact, always thought of himself as a gregarious man, or as gregarious as his position allowed. He had never knowingly missed the privacy afforded ordinary people or thought of their lives of anonymity as anything but a little sad.

Perhaps it was the isolation, but sitting in the vastness, gazing at the sky, he was suddenly aware of the overwhelming need to understand.

A small lizard scuttled past and interrupted his musings. The frantic patter of its feet on the sand disturbed the sleeping camel, which immediately started snorting in fright. It had already taken the twitchy animal an uncharacteristically long time to settle and the man was quickly at its side, reassuringly stroking its neck and speaking in hushed tones, even as the sounds of its distress echoed across the windless plain. The soothing seemed to work and soon the grunts petered away in to the rhythmic rasping of animal slumber. To keep the camel calm, he removed his saddle and unstrapped the heavy bag from its back, and took out his robe. In the distance a flock of sheep bleated in to the night.

The robe was thick and comforting, and he lay it down on the sand and curled it around him. He closed his eyes and tried to rest, but excitement and trepidation busied his mind. And, as always, with the seclusion of night came the doubts. What if this was simply a crisis of middle age or of a hungry imagination, he wondered. He wouldn't be the first of his family to search for a deeper meaning to his life amidst the frippery and shallowness of a pampered world. Or deep down was there a feeling that something else was at play? Throughout his journey, and, if he was honest, throughout his life, he was sure he had felt the irresistible touch of Time, pushing him forward, guiding him inexorably to this moment. And with this immutable force had steadily grown an awesome sense of destiny. Deep in the warmth of his robe, he shivered.

Unable to sleep, the man rolled on to his back and looked up at what had brought him here. The majestic sweep of the universe sparkled above him. He had looked at the sky before but in the smoky lights of the city and surrounded by his fussing retinue it had never quite looked like this. It was huge. It seemed to curve round the horizon itself. Everywhere the stars and their constellations bejewelled the night, twinkling as if dancing in celebration of the brightest of them all.

Yes, alone at times like this, a man could feel closer to God.

He remained staring skywards for another hour or so until his breathing slowed and his mind began to play, and sleep finally came. Alone in the enormity of the desert the light of the Star cradled him and kept him safe until daybreak stretched across the rose red landscape.

The man woke slowly from his dreaming and saddled up his own camel for the first time in his life. It was harder than it looked, but after some pulling and tugging it was done. Then, with a brief glance at the heavens, he kicked the royal beast and continued on his journey.

He had no notion of where he was going, but he knew the way.

TONY WILSON

1.
THE OLD MAN

In the city it was raining. Driving, slashing rain that stung the face and hunched the spine of those who struggled against it. It battered at the glass-fronted skyscrapers of the city centre and gunned down the busy thoroughfares in between, ricocheting along the twisting alleyways of the old town and clattering against its narrow, cobbled streets. The sky above was slate-grey and wintry, and the icy wind whipped spray off the river and lashed it in to sleet that slanted sharply in to those caught in the determined rush home. Water ran in streams along the kerbside, and where two streams met they swelled into huge puddles that filled every depression in the road and spread in the dark like black ink soaking across the tarmac.

The puddles struggled to make an impact as they splashed and splattered the countless unnoticing legs of the people hurrying home. At other times the puddles would have been an inconvenience; people would have stopped on the kerb, thought for a while, and then skirted round the side. This would have represented a deviation from the normal path home and a slowing, albeit measured in seconds, of the hurrying crowd. These lost seconds would ripple back along the commuter body, spreading as they went, adding minutes to the journey. Inevitably logjams would develop; people would stumble, tempers would be raised. The people at the back, blind to the hazard, would grow impatient and urge the horde forward. Pushing and shoving; shouting and cursing; grazes and bruises. Yes, on any other night puddles of this size demanded respect. But this was Christmas Eve, and it was everybody's right to be home at this time of year, and so puddles were ignored.

On a covered footbridge that spanned the main road a school choir sang of silent nights as the rain rattled along the glass walkway like a demented drummer trying to keep time with the carols being sung inside. Each child held a damp, cold candle in front of their beaming faces, all thrilled at being out so late and excited at the thought of tomorrow. Three Father Christmases, skin streaked with red dye from their cheap costumes, stood in puddles outside the station collecting for the blind. They rang their bells and shouted in the gale, but their yohohoing was lost on the wind. A mobile soup kitchen rocked so violently in the storm that occasionally the hot, thick broth being ladled in to the pots of those waiting patiently in the long queue would spill on to the hands of the unfortunate cradling the mug. The couple running the kitchen would apologise, but it was unnecessary; no one minded, no one complained.

The old man watched all this from his position under the huge Christmas tree in the forecourt of the station. He chuckled to himself as the rain poured through on to him, drenching his greatcoat and well-worn boots. Not such a great place to shelter after all, he thought. The brim of his hat, sodden and heavy, hung limply in front of his face and he pushed it aside and peered up at the tree, which was swaying violently in the wind.

The tree was hung with traditional white lanterns and baubles and enormous gold stars, and a twinkling, shifting rainbow haze hovered around it as the spray divided and coloured the light. A number of the stars had fallen off in the gale. Most of these rattled noisily in the corners of the station's cobbled forecourt, trapped there by the pounding wind, but some had been blown through the iron railings and down the side road before disappearing in to the dark, foaming waters of the river which flowed behind the station. The rest of the decorations hung precariously to their branches, pitching wildly back and forth with the rocking of the tree. The four cables of twisted steel fibres that wrapped around the tree's base and held it upright creaked and groaned as the thick trunk bowed first one way and then the other. Some of the grinding metal filaments had snapped and others had become dangerously worn, the old man noticed.

Time to go, he thought.

He peered out at the throng of commuters splashing through the rain and sighed. The rush hour would be over soon and the crowd would thin. Then it would be left to those hard at work and play to straggle home. And then would come the sad ones.

He pulled himself to his feet, his clothes soaked through but neither uncomfortable nor cold, and headed for the station. As he walked, the rainwater in his beard caught the light of the tree and sparkled. He ran his hand through the hair which grew untamed from his chin and a shower of droplets fell to the pavement, sending up a fine spray which glistened momentarily in the Christmas lights like stardust.

2.
DROWNING

Martin was drowning.

Or at least that's what it felt like. He seemed to have spent the last few years in a ceaseless and exhausting struggle to keep his head above the churning waters of his life. His business had sunk without trace four months ago, causing no end of hardship to himself and the nine staff he had been forced to let go. Most understood, but some, especially those with families to support, felt that it could have been saved if he had not devoted so much time to sinking his sorrows in drink. They were right, if a little harsh. He had no money to be speak of and even less prospects. His self esteem had largely floated away on the current of his misfortune and inevitably his health was suffering, submerged daily in diet of worry, whisky and junk food. In short, his life was a mess and had been since his young wife had died a few years before and left him with a small son, Christopher, and a sadness so heavy that, even now, if he stopped for a moment and allowed his mind to think about how much it hurt, he knew the despair would suck him down and close over his head like quicksand.

Grief may be invisible, but it has mass and form, he knew that, and it wrapped around his heart chaining him to his melancholy. Some days he felt like it was dragging every cell of his body down. Other times were more upbeat, but the quiet moments always came and when they did he would feel as impotent as Canute as a tide of guilt and regret rushed in and over him, draining him.

He was so tired. Many times at night he would lie awake listening in the dark to the dull rhythm of his heart, astounded that it could go on beating in a body so racked with fatigue. Occasionally he would drift off to sleep only to dream that his heart had stopped, and then he would suddenly wake in the cold, struggling for breath, until the rapid thudding on his breastbone resounded back in to his consciousness. He would then lie there, staring in to the blackness, the disappointment pressing down upon him. He needed help. He needed to be able to talk freely without feeling that his mind should be elsewhere; to genuinely enjoy something, anything, without mental comparison to another time; he needed to laugh heartily and to dance merrily; he needed to feel the potential for joy had not deserted him.

It had been like this for three years. Exactly three years, in fact. For it was on Christmas Eve three winters ago at twenty-five minutes past eight in the evening that his wife had finally succumbed to the cancer that had insidiously gnawed away at her body but not her spirit. And while it is true that everyone who is bereaved believes their loved one to have been goodness itself, in the case of Mary Downing it went beyond a mere truism. People spoke of her kindness and gentility as much before her death as after. Her courage in adversity was well known, although few could have guessed the depth of her strength. She never made any complaint of the pain with which the disease tormented her. Most said it was because the physical hurt was nothing compared to the agony of knowing that she would not see her little Christopher grow up and, most of all, to the realisation that she was leaving her beloved Martin alone. This was most difficult to bear. She knew he would find it hard, but did not guess how hard. She couldn't know she was leaving him drowning, with only his small son to bring him gasping to the surface.

As fate would have it, he was also drowning in a much more literal sense. Face down in a puddle in the corner of an alley, stinking of drink, he lay motionless as the storm water rose around him.

3.
THE SERGEANT

"For the last time Harris, I'm not comin'," said the Sergeant. "You do understand there's a war on, don't you?" he asked almost breathless with incredulity. "I think it's dishonourable and downright traitorous."

"Suit yerself, Sarge," replied Harris, unmoved. "I think it'll be alright. Most of the others are coming. They must miss it as much as we do. I'm going over." The young private rushed off along the trench, his heavy boots crunching the frozen mud underfoot. "Merry Christmas, Sarge," he shouted, his voice trailing in the distance. "Yer miserable old git," he added when he was far enough.

"Going over? What do these lads know about going over?" the Sergeant muttered to himself in his clipped Scottish brogue. He watched the young soldier run from the trench, and his thin, pinched face, pock marked by nineteen years of military service, looked momentarily sad. Eventually, he shrugged and turned away.

He boiled up some greyish water on the Tommy stove in the middle of the dugout and made himself a mug of weak tea. The Sergeant was still getting used to having it without sugar. Supplies had deemed it a luxury item available only to commissioned officers, and even Sergeant Nethercote, who had begged and borrowed just about everything from the Army stores in twenty-two years of service life, could not lay his hands on any of the precious white granules.

He sat his broad, bony frame down on an old ammunition box which doubled as a stool and cupped his long fingers around the hot tin mug. It was quiet. He closed his eyes and inhaled deeply. The feel of the warm metal against his chilled hands and the bland smell of the tea were familiar and comforting sensations; they belonged to a world he understood in a time that grew increasingly beyond his understanding. He sipped the insipid brew through the gaps in his teeth and drew the liquid noisily over his tongue. At least the war would cure him of his sweet tooth, he reflected.

The muffled sound of an explosion several miles away interrupted his reverie and dragged him back to a world at war. He thought of the enthusiastic Private Harris and shook his head. Every month they sent him forty fresh-faced boys and he had to try to teach them the art of modern warfare, and how to survive it, before they got their turn to 'go over'. Then they sent him some more. Most had signed up to escape the drudgery of the factories or simply to be sure of the next meal. They were invariably disappointed. Tedium and hunger were almost bigger enemies in the trenches than the Germans. Almost.

Of course, some had come brimming full of patriotism, expecting to play for glory on a muddy, bloodless field. Well they got the mud, alright. But what they did not foresee, could not have imagined, was the absolute horror of it all. This war was beyond even the most nightmarish thoughts of a young lad from the grime and green fields of home. Certainly no recruiting officer ever mentioned the machine guns or their barbarous efficiency, even though it meant that over half of them would be cut down within yards of their first and final glorious charge. Neither did they talk of the unceasing noise of the whizz bangs exploding over head, the numbing fatigue of sleeplessness, the dirt, the rain, the cold, the stench of death. In all his years of service the Sergeant had never encountered such an evil as this war and his hatred for those who had unleashed it was deep and unbounded. At night he still thought of Ypres.

"Good evening, Sergeant," said the new subaltern. "I trust you have seen what's happening?"

"Yes, sir."

"And do you approve?"

"No, sir. No I do not."

"Mm, neither do I, I suppose," said the subaltern uncertainly. They stood in awkward silence for several seconds. "Do you think it will do any harm? It is Christmas, after all," he asked.

The Sergeant considered this. "They're young lads, sir, so they don't think about things too deeply, but they need to keep in mind what we're fighting for. There's good and there's bad in this war. We're not the ones who choke armies with mustard gas or murder babies or bomb civilians. It wasn't us who decided we wanted to be emperors of Europe and dragged honest men away from their wives and families. They're the cause of all this - this badness, sir. We must never lose sight of that."

"Quite so, quite so," said the subaltern, taken aback by the Sergeant's forcefulness. He peered out to where the fires had been lit. "Still, better keep it quiet from the top brass, eh?" he said and wandered off.

The subaltern was only twenty years old and was the third in as many months. They said this one had been called in off his honeymoon and had not even had time to complete his training. The Sergeant watched the new man stumble along the trench, tripping over boxes and sleeping men, a man far from home. The regiment would almost certainly be calling for another subaltern soon. More telegrams, more tears.

The Sergeant fumbled for the cushion his wife had made for him on his last trip home. He missed her. It was a strange and alien feeling for him and he had no notion of how to deal with it. He wondered if it was the same for her or whether her youth made it easier to cope. Without thinking, he ran his hands through his close cropped hair, thinner that it was and already greying at the sides.

He removed the paper in which he kept the cushion wrapped and brushed his fingers along the lace edges. Not much of a married life, so far, he reflected. They'd only been married four months when the war started and most of that time had been taken up with training. Still, she knew he was a career soldier when she met him, and it did have its advantages. It was the Army, after all, who had paid for their stylish military wedding in Bannockburn. He had looked very grand in his kilt and she'd held his hand tightly as they danced through the raised regimental swords outside the church. As ever, she'd looked beautiful in her ivory wedding dress and he was grateful he'd been able to give her the sort of wedding she deserved.

His men did him proud that day, draping the occasion with as much pomp as the townsfolk had seen. Even captains Campbell and McCallum had come along to wish him well. They had looked handsome and noble in their mess kit and spent most of the evening surrounded by the young women of the town. They were proper Scottish gentlemen and he wished he was under their command now. Sadly, Captain Campbell was killed at Ypres and Captain McCallum had been badly burnt in France and was in the process of being invalided back to Edinburgh. Rumour had it that he had also lost an arm. The young women's eyes would pass him by now.

"We came back to get you, Sarge," puffed the regiment's two cooks suddenly appearing at the dugout entrance. They were both sweating and out of breath. "Thought you could do with the exercise," they grinned.

"No, lads, best do without me," muttered the Sergeant.

"Oh c'mon, Sarge. Most of the others are there and they're all asking for you," said the older of the two.

"Look lads, I know you mean well, but it's not for me, okay?" he growled. He could feel himself beginning to tense.

"Don't be silly, Sarge. You'll enjoy it. And we've promised the boys we'd get you, so we're can't go back without you, can we?!" jollied the younger one.

The Sergeant turned on them. "No, no, no. For the last bloody time, no," he shouted, "I'll not be comin'. I don't like it, I don't like it at all, and I'll have nothing to do with the whole sick affair. I've told just about everyone else and now I've told you. Right, now go away and leave me in peace."

"Oh no, Sarge, c'mon," continued the younger one, undaunted. "It'll be a laugh. It'll certainly be different." They both chuckled. "And it is Christmas. You know, peace on Earth, goodwill to all men, and all that."

"Yeah, forgive and forget, eh?" ventured the other, half in jest. The Sergeant winced. "Well just for now," he added hurriedly.

The Sergeant looked up at them. The two cooks were, as tradition demands, the only ones in the trenches who carried any excess weight. No one begrudged them their extra rations; they did a good job with impossibly meagre resources. And they were good lads, inseparable most of the time and always laughing.

They were smiling now as they stood in the doorway of the dugout waiting for the Sergeant to respond. He could see them grinning through the cloud of freezing breath that wreathed around their faces and dripped coldly on to their flushed cheeks.

He began slowly and with unmistakable menace.

"You have two choices, boys. You can either get out of my sight now and never, and I mean never, mention it again." Deliberately he reached in to his kit and unsheathed his bayonet. "Or I can take this bayonet and skewer you both through the heart and then boil you in that soggy muck that you somehow had the nerve to call Christmas puddin'."

The two cooks' eyes widened. Their faces were set in an awkward half grin, frozen there by a mixture of fear and surprise.

The Sergeant stared fixedly at them both, stabbing at the air with his bayonet; even in the dark it looked razor sharp and lethal.

"But ..," began the younger of the two. All further protestations were abruptly stopped by the slap of the older cook's hand across his mouth.

"We'll be off then, Sarge," he said pulling the younger man by the shoulder. They scampered back along the trench and pulled themselves up in to the clear night, thankful to be back in the safety of no-man's land.

The Sergeant watched them through unfocusing eyes, dimly aware of the blood flowing back in to his body from his tense limbs. He shivered. He had not meant to be so rough, but could not help himself. It was an unnerving feeling. He was used to being in control.

He laid the bayonet down on the cushion and momentarily looked at his hand. Kids, he thought, he was fighting kids now. Sadly they were only young by virtue of their age. People grew up swiftly in the trenches. Many spoke of a generation being lost, of a world emptied of young men, but the only young men left in this war were the ones who had just arrived. Dysentry, trenchfoot, lice and fatigue could wizen a teenage body in weeks, and the carnage and hopelessness soon suffocated even the most youthful of spirits. And the mind? Well that had no chance. He'd come to believe that madness was not the easy way out that they'd been encouraged to think. It wasn't the strong or the brave who survived with their senses intact, it was the mindless. The sight of life being ripped out in an instant by shells which shredded limbs to stumps or made eyeballs blow or left ears ringing and useless, could render the most hardy of men a stranger to reason. Yes, sometimes he thought insanity was the only possible refuge of the intellect in this war.

"Yer not going, Jock?" piped Sergeant Nethercote, his head craning in to the dugout.

"Don't you start, Maggy or I swear I'll kill you. I've cleaned my pistol and I'm itchin' to use it, German or no."

"Okay, okay, calm down. Blimey, are you on edge."

"Achh," shrugged the Sergeant. "I've just had enough, that's all. And I nae want to hear any more about it."

"Fine by me. I won't mention it again. Honest," said Nethercote taken aback. "Bit touchy, aren't you, Jock. And hardly brimmin' with Christmas spirit."

"And I'm sick of people going on about Christmas bleedin' spirit, about it being a special day," the Sergeant exploded. "A day of forgiving and forgetting. What's the point of forgetting for a day, I ask yer? Does it make you any happier? Does it bring any one back? It's bad enough being out here at Christmas away from, well you know, everyone at home, without person after person, most just outta nappies, pestering me with advice regarding moral conduct. I'll be nice when I want to be nice, and I'll forgive who I want to forgive. Do I make myself clear?!"

"Strewth, Jock. I was only comin' in to offer you a Christmas tipple," said Maggy, pulling a bottle of scotch out of his duffle bag. He had earned the soubriquet Maggy - or Magpie - for his ability to steal, horde and distribute things, anything, for a price. Christmas was a time of great opportunities for a man like Sergeant Nethercote. "I didn't expect an ear bashing."

"Well, what did you expect with all this going on, eh?" the Sergeant shouted, waving his arms. He paused. He was breathing heavily. "And where did you get that from, you thieving git. You know it's against regulations. How can the men respect you when you steal from our own stores, eh? And if they don't respect you, they won't follow you. And if the don't follow you, well, people get hurt. You know that. These kids get killed. What sort of person are you that yer thieve from your own side, anyway? I've a good mind to put you on a charge for pilfering."

"Bloody 'ell, Jock. What are you goin' on about? Listen to you, will ya. I came round 'ere to wish you Merry Christmas and 'ave a small drink with an old comrade-in-arms, even if you are a miserable Scottish sod, and this is the thanks I get, a bloody lecture on duty and warfare. They all said you've been a bit strange lately, but bleedin' 'ell, Jock. I'm off." Nethercote picked up the bottle and turned to go. The Sergeant caught him by the arm and gripped tightly.

"No, don't Maggy, don't go. Stay pal. Look, I'm - I'm sorry. Please stay."

Nethercote was not an unkind man and twenty-two years of stealing had helped him not to take offence easily.

""Sorry" and "please" in the same sentence, Jock? Blimey, it must be Christmas." Nethercote said dryly. They both smiled. "You can let go now, Jock. I'm not going anywhere," he said, nodding to the Sergeant's hold on his arm. The Sergeant's knuckles were white.

"Aye, right enough." The Sergeant released his grip. For a few seconds he looked at his open hand, inspecting it as if it was part of another body.

"Drink, Jock?" asked Nethercote, holding up the bottle of scotch. The Sergeant was staring at the ground. He nodded. "Stolen whisky, okay. I'm sorry, there's only a fieving git for company."

Nethercote pulled two champagne flutes out of his ubiquitous duffle bag and held them up for the Sergeant's approval. The Sergeant half smiled and shrugged. "Right sit down and let's 'ave a drink, then."

They pulled up a box each and Nethercote filled both glasses to the brim. They drank in silence. Nethercote shuffled awkwardly, seemingly mindful that he should say something. "Just like old times, eh?" he managed.

"It's beginning to grind on me, Maggy," resumed the Sergeant without answering. "Starting to get me down, it is. P'haps people like me and you are just too long in the tooth for changing. P'haps not. Other times might have been different. Egypt, Sudan, India. Maybe. It just seemed so different then, more manageable, not as nasty. It certainly wasn't like it is here, was it, Maggy?" implored the Sergeant.

"Well, it was 'otter," replied the struggling Nethercote. The Sergeant gave him a bewildered look. "This war's not like any other we've fought, I'll grant you that," he offered.

"It's not like any other there's ever been," corrected the Sergeant, his voice beginning to tremor. "Other campaigns were a picnic compared to this. They were like quarrels between friends. There were rules. No-one much got hurt. This is different. This is, this is," his words trailed off. "This is hell."

The Sergeant bit his lip and tried to calm down. He looked down and realised his hands were shaking. He was normally a phlegmatic man and these outbursts of emotion were unsettling him.

"They want me to forget?" he said quietly. "It's only my memory that keeps me going."

Out in the darkness of no-man's land, away from the fires and undetected by both sides, an enemy crept towards the trenches, yet another in this war with only his memory to keep him going.

4.
THE TRAIN

The old man walked along the platform with an ease belying his years. He should have shuffled; with his rheumatic limbs and shoulders hunched with age, and in the grand tradition of those advanced in years battling against inclement weather, he most definitely should have shuffled. But shuffle he did not; nor trudge, nor clamber, nor limp, nor wearily pull. He simply walked, with no trace of the burden of time or the debility of ill health.

At the last carriage on the most distant platform, the old man stopped. There was no one around. He stood facing the carriage and peered to his right at the main station concourse in the distance; nothing but the echoes of celebrations. He looked to his left along the open line and over the bridge that spanned the river and beyond; the wind, rain and sleet continued to buffet the track, but there was no sign of anyone. He was alone. Smiling to himself, he raised his arms above his head and brought them swiftly down to his side describing a rough circle.

Gazing upon the scene, a distant onlooker would have seen an old man made cold and wet by the rain trying to warm himself. The guard sitting on the train opposite, tired, bored and out of the old man's sight, saw something similar, but what he *felt* was entirely different. Put simply, he felt a change. Not a grand or moving sensation, just an awareness that momentarily something had shifted, as if an invisible plane had jetted past and the carriage had been sucked for an instant in to its slipstream. And at the very limits of his hearing, both in terms of distance and sound, his ears registered a dull low thud, like a heartbeat from the beginning of Time.

In the immediate aftermath the guard noticed the old man sitting laughing to himself on the darkened train, although when picking over the event later in his mind he realised he had no memory of him actually getting on.

5.
MARTIN

It was cold and damp in his bedroom. Yet another thing he would have to sort out. The house was only three years old but the roof leaked, the heating was hopeless and the plumbing needed fixing. More pressures. He wished he could just leave it all and go somewhere far away, somewhere warm. Of course, that wasn't going to happen. He had responsibilities, and a son. It really was cold in here.

There was a noise. Martin walked out in to the corridor. The carpets were soaked with water and squelched as his bare feet moved over them. He hadn't noticed that before. Also, the plaster seemed to be peeling badly from around the door frames. He'd have to call the builder again in the morning. The poor man must be sick of him.

The noise again. What was that? Hard to tell exactly where it was coming from. Sounded like it was upstairs, but couldn't be sure in this house; it made strange noises all the time. Probably just a floorboard, or the wind, or a mouse. He leant against the wall and realised that water was trickling down the plaster and the paint was beginning to run. It stained one sleeve of his coat a vivid crimson. Strange.

Then suddenly it came again. Indistinct, muffled by the damp, swallowed by the sodden walls, but unmistakeably a cry for help. Martin ran to Christopher's bedroom and slammed the door open. The room was empty. He frantically searched under the bed and in the small wardrobe, but his son was not there. A sickly taste appeared in his mouth, sour and acrid. Water was seeping up through the floorboards and forming puddles in the corners of the room.

He rushed back in to the corridor and shouted for his son, and froze, bewildered and terrified. No voice; he had no voice. His mouth was open, his brain was engaged but he could make no sound. He staggered backwards in shock. Shock. Yes, that was it, he was in shock. He relaxed and tried again, but once more, he was struck mute; no whisper, no croak, no sound at all. The fear swelled rapidly within him. Gathering his strength, he screamed his son's name once more, screamed until his vocal chords were hoarse with effort and the sinews of his neck stuck out grostesquely like the swollen roots of a tree, but still the only noise he could hear was the sound of rushing water, which was now pouring down through the corniced ceiling and beginning to fill the house like a gigantic tank. The pressure in Martin's head overwhelmed him and he fell backwards in to the rapidly rising levels of the deluge.

The cold revived him. He managed to steady himself in the chest-high freezing water and closed his eyes, listening for his son's voice. Nothing. A pair of boy's football boots floated past. Where was he? He could not lose him. Not again, sweet Jesus, not again.

And then it came. Clear and resonating, as if shouted across a frozen pond on a still winter's day. The cacophony of the flood was suddenly silent as his son's voice came bouncing across the surface of the water like a skimming stone.

The attic. He was in the attic.

Relief warmed Martin momentarily. Breathing was still difficult. The water was rising quickly and he was now treading water with his head only a few feet from the ceiling. He must reach Christopher. Again, he heard his son call. Still desperate, but somehow changed. Not scared for himself. Martin began to gasp. The exertion must have tired him more than he thought. He was struggling for air. The water was now pressing his head against the ceiling and he was treading furiously with his neck craned backwards sucking in the few remaining inches of air. Still time. He must reach his son. The attic door, where was it ?

Cold enveloped him as the water suddenly covered his head. He held his breath but his lungs were already screaming. This was it. His son was going to lose him. He was going to be alone. Tears peeled from Martin's open eyes and hung like pearls in the dirty brown water, and life began to slip away.

Suddenly, through the water, a voice. Christopher's voice. Calling, urging. Scared not for himself; a cry for help for his father. A light came on and Christopher's hand pulled him up in to the attic, in to the light, with uncommon strength.

6.
TOM AND VIC

"You okay, mate?" shouted the stranger, as he pulled Martin on to his back.

Martin coughed and heaved as he fought for air. Rainwater spat from his mouth and nose. His chest burnt.

"Take it easy, you've been nose down in the rain for God knows 'ow long," the man continued, his sparse yellow teeth chattering in the cold. He took a swig from the bottle he held in his partially gloved hand and added, "you're lucky we was 'ere."

"Is 'e alright?" shouted the other tramp from a doorway across the alley.

"Well, 'e's alive," yelled the man, "but 'e's not looking well." He glanced down at Martin and frowned. "He'll be fine soon enough, though," he hollered by way of encouragement.

Martin had come staggering along the tiny backstreet some minutes earlier, rebounding off the walls like a human pinball. Coat flailing and hopelessly incoherent, he had eventually tripped on the rubbish piled outside the back of the restaurant where the two tramps had set up camp and had fallen head first against the cheap, jagged, pebble-dash of the cafe next door.

"D'you know where you are, mate?" asked the tramp. "You came tumblin' down 'ere about ten minutes ago. You've 'ad a fall. You must 'ave passed out or somethin'."

Martin said nothing. He felt too ill to respond. Slowly and painfully, he clambered off the fetid pile of wet bread and half opened cans on which he found himself. Two well-chewed chicken drumsticks stuck to the sleeve of his coat and he brushed them away with a practised and unthinking flick of the hand. He had no idea where he was. How he had got there, he could guess; experience had robbed him of any sense of surprise on these occasions.

"Okay, easy does it, lad. That was quite a knock you took," cautioned the tramp, taking another sip from his bottle. The tramp's mouth was dry despite the drink and little flakes of skin tore from his cracked lips as he struggled to make himself heard. The alleyway's walls were high and the shrill wind whined through its passage, numbing any exposed parts.

The rain pounded unnoticed in to Martin as he struggled on to all fours, wincing. Above him the storm roared and the heavens cracked spectacularly with lightning. The bright silver flashes briefly illuminated Martin's ghostly grimacing face as he began to vomit. The tramp looked on sympathetically.

"Take yer time, son, take yer time," he said kindly. "It'll pass soon enough. Just keep your 'ead down and breathe through yer nose." He put a hand on Martin's shoulder. It was wet and very cold.

"Deep breaths, mister. Get some air in to ya and then come in 'ere out of the rain for a bit," recommended the other tramp from the warmth of the doorway. "Bring 'im in, Tom. When he's well enough," he added with the air of someone who was more than happy to do a good turn for those in need as long as no effort was required on his part.

Tom, who was still leaning over Martin giving an occasional well-meaning pat on the back, looked up incredulously. The wind howled around the narrow alley.

Martin's breathing gradually became less laboured as his immediate illness passed, but it was only a brief respite. The smell of his sickness was so foul that it made him wretch further, sending such violent and repeated spasms through his body, it was as if the lightning itself was prodding him. The vomit splashed on his hands and ran in thick lava-like streams in to the drains on the back of the storm water. He wished he was dead.

"You're lucky to be 'ere," offered Tom. "We've only been 'ere a week or so. No-one else around to find ya. You're a lucky man, definite."

Still Martin said nothing. He was shivering violently but showed no inclination to move. The side of his face was grazed from the fall and blood was seeping through the thin skin. He let it drip to the ground.

Tom looked down at his numb fingers. The tips were blue.

"Son, this night's what we call a murder night. It's not a good night to be outside. Believe me, it's not a good night at all." Still no response. "Look, if we don't get inside, I'm gonna die of pneumonia and what sort of Christmas present would that be, eh?" he tried, but to no avail.

"Come an' give me a 'and, will yer Vic? It's bleedin' freezing and the lad won't move," shouted Tom, apparently concluding that Martin's instincts for self survival were not as well-honed as his.

"What?" mimed Victor with his hand cupped against his ear.

"We need to pull 'im up and get 'im out of the cold."

Victor shook his head in mock incomprehension and pulled his padded blanket of cardboard and polythene further up his body. Tom shrugged his shoulders and put his bottle of drink down on the wet, black concrete. He slipped his hands under Martin's shoulders and whispered "C'mon son, 'elp us out 'ere," and heaved him to his feet.

The sounds of Tom's back cracking could be heard above the wind.

"It was a miracle we 'eard you," said Tom after they had got Martin settled in the shelter of the doorway, "what wiv the weather an' all."

"Bloody miracle," repeated Victor.

They had wrapped Martin in an old blanket that Tom used for laying underneath his cardboard bed to temper the cold of the stones. It was tattered and smelt of damp but it was warm and the first tinges of life began to creep back in to Martin's body.

"I tell yer, you would 'ave been a gonner if we'd 'ave left it much longer. Drowning, you were, blowing bubbles through yer nose by the time I got to ya."

"Thanks," Martin uttered in a non-committal way.

The two men looked at each other. Martin saw their expressions.

"No, really, thanks. I mean it. I - I just feel like shit, that's all." He reached in to his coat pocket and pulled out his mobile phone. It had a deep crack across its face and was as dark as the night. He cursed.

"'S'alright son," said Tom, "you're bound to feel a little worse for wear. You were quite tanked up," he chuckled. "Celebrating were ya?"

Martin put the broken mobile back in to his coat and stared down at the wet paving stones. "Hardly," he whispered.

"O well, don't worry, you can stay 'ere for as long as you like."

Victor's eyes suddenly widened in admonition.

"Well, until you gets yer bearings back, I mean," Tom quickly corrected. "I don't s'pose you'll want to stay that long, anyway," he added, looking around. "Still, it's warm and dry, the company's fair and it's open all night," he laughed.

Martin looked at the stairwell. The black iron steps were old and weather beaten; they had no doubt seen many a night like this. The cheap charcoal paint had peeled at the corners and rust was eating away at the exposed metal. Some steps had weakened and twisted with the weight of time and rain fell from them in an unending stream of drips and formed a watery bead curtain in front of the doorway that was Tom and Victor's home.

Victor followed Martin's gaze. "Not bad, eh?" he piped.

31

It was dirty and damp and had been for years, but there were signs that the two men had tried to eek out a semblance of comfort here. There was an upturned crate that was used as a table. Several new aluminium foil dishes lay on top, remnants of a soup kitchen's Christmas specials, Martin guessed. The plastic knives and forks that came with the food were stored in a glass by the side. Several empty cans of beer were strewn across the area but there were also neat piles of rubbish dotted here and there where they had clearly made the occasional effort to tidy up. Their two beds were a series of flattened cardboard boxes wrapped in polythene and thickened with fresh newspapers. At the back of the doorway were two black bin liners brimming with bric-a-brac and old clothes and holes. These were the possessions of Tom and Victor.

"I do appreciate your help," said Martin, somewhat guiltily. "Sorry, if I seemed a bit ungrateful." He then added a little awkwardly, "How long have you been here?"

"'bout a fortnight," Vic chirpily replied.

"And no-one bothers you?"

"No. Young lad who owns the shop said we was fine to stay 'ere for a bit."

"Well, he never actually said we could stay," interjected Tom. "He just didn't kick us out."

"Same thing," affirmed Vic.

Martin got the impression that in Vic's mind this was as good as a gold-embossed invitation to come on over and stay for the holidays. Martin thought of the young shop owner, brimming with youthful success, opening up his store in the morning and finding two old men sleeping out the back in the wet and cold. No wonder he'd been reluctant to get rid of them. Martin wondered what he would have done in the same situation. If he still had a business to open, that is.

"Feeling better now, son?" asked Tom. "You look a bit brighter. More colour in yer cheeks."

"Yes thanks. Certainly warmer," Martin replied. "Thanks for the blanket."

"You need it on nights like these."

"Gotta 'ave a blanket," seconded Vic.

There was silence for a few moments. Martin pulled the blanket closer round him.

"What's a murder night?" he asked.

"Sorry?" replied Vic.

"A murder night. You mentioned it earlier," replied Martin, nodding to Tom. "You said it's what you called a night like tonight."

Tom sighed. "It's when the weather's like this," he said waving to the pelting, freezing rain slanting in to the alleyway. "So cold and wet it stings. Means one or two of the boys will be gone in the morning."

"Gone?" asked Martin, momentarily unclear.

"Yep, you know, gone," replied Tom softly.

"At least their Christmas will be warm," Vic added with an air of resignation.

Martin looked at the tramps, at a loss at what to say.

"You don't want some water, do you?" asked Vic brightly, holding up an old, dented bottle of mineral water. "One of the lads from the restaurant filled it up for us yesterday."

"Sorry? O, no, not sure," replied Martin, a touch hesitantly. "Could I stick to whisky, if you don't mind," he added nodding to the three quarters full bottle of scotch next to Tom's bed. "Don't want to mix my drinks."

Tom smiled. "Well, we was going to save this till tomorrow, but what the hell. It's nearly time and you look like you could do wiv a bit of Christmas spirit." Tom unscrewed the top of the whisky bottle and went to take a swig. " 'ere's to you son," he declared. Victor shot up his hand to stop him.

"Use the glasses, you dirty ole bugger. It is Christmas, after all," announced Victor. "And we've got company," he added motioning to the younger man.

"Yeah, right, Vic. I was forgetting me manners. Sorry, son."

"Martin's the name".

"Oh right, Martin. I'm Tom. And this is Vic."

"Vic-tor," he corrected.

Victor cast around in his bag of belongings and fished out a packet of four clear plastic beakers. "Riverboat Christmas disco. Last year. Eventful," explained Tom with a smile. One was cracked and Victor put this to one side. He poured a little water in to each of the remaining three, swished it around in an effort to clear away the dust and offered them to Tom with as much ceremony as the situation allowed. After a moment's hesitation and with eyebrows raised Tom filled each to the brim.

"It's a little early, but Happy Christmas to you both," said Tom raising his glass.

"And a 'appy Christmas to you, mate," replied Victor, glass aloft, "and a merry one to you, Martin."

They both looked at Martin. He sat in silence staring out past the rain. However, much he tried, he could not forget.

"Martin," urged Victor with a degree of annoyance, "'appy Christmas."

"Oh sorry, yeah, Happy Christmas." The words stung his throat, they always did. He raised his glass. "To you both, Tom and Victor." They nodded. "Sorry, I lost myself for a bit there. Thanks for the drink."

They supped in silence.

"Miles away were yer?" asked Tom.

"Yeah, just a little," stuttered Martin, rubbing his eyes.

"Don't worry, son, I spend most of my life miles away," assured Tom in a tone of gentle understanding. He sipped at his drink. "You couldn't stay 'ere otherwise."

Martin looked around at the stinking alleyway and at the damp doorway under the crumbling stairwell that was Tom's home. He felt ashamed.

Tom saw Martin's expression. "Coming 'ome's always a bit of a bugger, though," he added in a matter-of-fact way.

"The knack is," laughed Victor shaking the whisky bottle at Martin, "not to come back too often." He lifted his glass and downed it in one gulp. "So, as I said, Happy Christmas," he chuckled and motioned to Tom to do the same.

After a moment's introspection, Tom smiled and said, "Yep, you really don't want to be hanging around 'ere for the 'olidays, so..." he downed his whisky and wiped his lips. "Happy bloody Christmas, Martin."

"Yes, I see your point. All the very best to you both on your travels."

In a moment he had drunk the whisky and was offering it for a refill.

7.

WAR

The Sergeant took his boot off the German's neck. A quick search had revealed a knife and a small regimental issue handgun, which the Sergeant quickly threw away. They were on the outer reaches of the frozen track of ground that separated the two sides and the weapons bounced unheard and unseen in to the night.

"So what are you up to then, eh?" the Sergeant sneered. "Spying? Murdering? Bidding us a very German Merry Christmas?"

The soldier looked up at the Sergeant and blinked rapidly several times, struggling to focus. He seemed dazed and in some distress.

"I asked, what are you up to?" growled the Sergeant.

There was no response. The German's face was twisted, as if in pain, and his eyes darted wildly side to side. Blood trickled from his ears.

"I'm warning you, sonny. Don't try my patience."

The Sergeant had spotted the German crawling slowly towards the British lines minutes earlier. After his talk with Maggy, he had walked to the very limits of the trenches to collect his thoughts, and finish the scotch, and had seen the shadow of stealthy movement about fifty yards away.

The prostrate soldier had capitulated without a fight. Quite what he had hoped to achieve with such feeble weaponry was of only passing interest to the Sergeant who saw this as yet another example of the nefarious nature of the German psyche. To launch a spy and potential assassin on this day of all days, when men's thoughts were of home and God, was typical of this enemy and this war. Even in such barbaric times civilised countries tried to keep to certain principles of humanity. The Sergeant's experiences in other theatres of war were peppered with examples of the essential decency of the enemy: prisoners were treated fairly; treaties were adhered to; promises kept. It made war less brutal without detracting from the simple heroism of the whole endeavour. But this conflict had been different from the start. Conventions were ignored and rules broken and dipped in blood. It was as if the devil had come across a group of fat boys playing marbles for a bag of sweets and had given them each an axe and told them the last one alive gets the prize.

"Don't tell me you can't speak English," blasted the Sergeant, holding the soldier by his tattered collar. A fine spittle sprayed from his mouth on to the German's face. "What do yer take me for? They wouldn't have sent you over here on a night like this if you did nae speak the lingo, eh? No point spying on people when you cannae understand what they're talking about, is there? I said, is there?"

The German visibly recoiled at the Sergeant's breath, but the Briton's grip was unbreakable. The scotch had stripped away the thin crust of restraint from the Sergeant's volcanic emotions and the blistering anger boiling underneath was exposed. Unable to escape the Sergeant's grasp, the prisoner turned his head rapidly back and forth, staring emptily in to the darkness.

"Didn't bank on getting caught, did ye?" spat the Sergeant, pulling the prisoner towards him. "Don't roll your eyes at me, lad. I know shell shock when I see it. I've seen enough to fill a hundred nuthouses. Thanks to you." He threw the German down on to the frozen, spiky earth. "Just answer the questions. Answer them and things will be better for you." The soldier made no response. "Talk to me, damn you."

Seemingly oblivious to the Sergeant's mounting fury, the soldier lay on the ground, panting heavily and mumbling in his native tongue.

"In English, Fritz. In English," snarled the Sergeant. "I know you can speak it. I know you can. Speak bloody English now or, I'm warning you, you'll regret it." The Sergeant leant down towards the prisoner. "Sie sprechen English," he growled in an accent as harsh and jagged as a Highland crag.

The German's eyes flickered, as if something registered. He squinted at the Sergeant then looked down at his own uniform. It was torn down the front and his chest was badly lacerated. He shook his head painfully, as if trying to hear clearly in the silence.

"No? Right. You are now a prisoner of the British Army. You will be tried on charges of spying for the enemy and, given the seriousness of the offence, will no doubt be shot at His Majesty's pleasure. This, of course, will be too good for you. But this is the British Army and you will be given a fair trial. You may be surprised to learn that you will not be tortured or beaten. You will be given the same sickly muck we have to eat and you will be able to dress properly and wash with the same bucket of frozen water as the rest of us. You will at all times be treated decently and as a human being. Undoubtedly this will be hard for you to reason but in the end, Fritz, take it from me you will be shot. Understand? Verstehen?" shouted the Sergeant, leaning forward so his face was inches from his captive's.

The soldier gazed around him, bewilderment etched in to his features, then rubbed his face furiously with his hands. He winced in pain. His hands were bloodied and sore and he held them up in front of him, turning them round under the starry sky.

"Put your hands down," warned the Sergeant. "Down, I say. They've done enough damage, already. Your gassing and machine gunning days are over now, my Krauty friend." The captive lowered his arms to his side and then suddenly looked up, his eyes wide and clear, his face frozen in horror. "O, you understand now do you ?"

Without warning, the German began to thrash wildly around on the ground and tried to crawl away. He made about a yard. The Sergeant's boot came down on his neck with the force of a tank and pinned him to the dirt.

"You sneaky, schemin' Hun scum. You ungrateful bastard. Most of the others woulda given you a bloody good hiding by now. Have I done that? Have I?"

The Sergeant lifted his pistol behind him and whipped it down to within an inch of the soldier's cheekbone. The German tensed at the expected blow, but it never came. Instead the handle of the gun shuddered against his face as the Sergeant fought to overcome his instincts.

"No," the Sergeant growled to himself, eyes fixated on his violently shaking hand just a whisker from the soldier's face. "No," he grunted again, louder this time. His breathing was racing and his face swollen with fury as he battled for self control. The German stayed hunched over, a look of terror spread across the lines of his bloody face.

Suddenly, the Sergeant dropped his arm to his side, lifted his head to the heavens and screamed, "God damn this war!"

The sound echoed across the frozen wastes of no-man's land and carried in to the trenches and in to the dugouts of those toasting Christmas, and continued over the unmarked graves behind. Something stirred. Away in the middle where the fires were burning the noise went unnoticed amongst the fray.

The German cowered on the ground, shaking violently and uncontrollably. His hands were cupped over the sides of his head, as if trying to block out the pain of the Sergeant's screams.

"Okay, then," said the Sergeant regaining a degree of composure, "let's do this properly. Right, who are you?"

The Sergeant reached around the soldier's neck for an identification tag. The German backed away in fright, but the

Sergeant's boot held him firm. There was no tag, so the Sergeant looked in the half torn breast pocket of the soldier's tunic and grew suddenly pale.

"Ypres? You were at Ypres?" he said, looking at the small, star-shaped bronze campaign medal bearing the name of the Belgian battleground that was loosely pinned to the soldier's ragged uniform. "You were there? You were out there, on the other side?" he asked, as the name conjured up barely repressed memories of carnage and horror. "Oh sweet Jesus."

In an instant, the strength appeared to pour away from the Sergeant's body and he released his grip on the captive. The change in mood was so sudden, it appeared to frighten the soldier even more and he immediately curled himself in to a ball in clear expectation of a beating.

"Oh God. Oh dear God," muttered the Sergeant, sagging to the ground. Gently and without a sound, the Sergeant cradled his head in his hands and began to rock back and forth, his mind buzzing with flashes of a place which part of him had never left.

For several minutes all was silent. Then, slowly and carefully, the German took his arms away from his head and glanced briefly at the Sergeant. A confused look played on the prisoner's face. The Sergeant was swaying to and fro, head down, consumed completely by his memories. The only sound was of the soft rhythmic cracking of the rutted ground as the Sergeant rocked across the soil. The soldier turned away for a few moments and then looked back again, but the Sergeant's demeanour remained unaltered. A nervous tic tugged at the prisoner's face. He lay backwards and stared at the sky for a few minutes, then kicked the hard ground with the heel of his boot and a soft thud reverberated in to the still night air; the Sergeant neither lifted his head, nor responded in any way. Breathing heavily now, the German slowly sat upright and squinted at the Sergeant, as if trying to work out whether his agonies were real or some ghastly affectation. A decision seemingly made, the soldier began to slowly uncoil his legs which were crusty with blood. He grimaced as he brought them painfully underneath him. Little dark patches spotted and spread on the torn khaki of his trousers, like the first droplets of a storm, as scabs ruptured and sores seeped. Gradually he pulled himself in to a half crouch position and as he did so the frozen ground scraped underneath, puncturing the silence. He turned and stared at the Sergeant. There was no reaction; the Sergeant appeared oblivious to everything but the images raging in his head. The German girded himself, slowly took his weight through his arms and tensed his muscles.

"It started out as a normal operation," said the Sergeant suddenly raising his head. The German visibly shrunk and sank to the dirt.

"We bombarded them with shells all night, and all night we sat and watched. Nervous, excited. 'bout an hour before dawn we finally got the message to attack, go over the top. The machine guns were all either disabled or destroyed, we were told, and the battle would be over within the hour." The Sergeant's eyes were on the German, but he was looking elsewhere. He continued flatly, "It was the first campaign of the war and it was all exciting and new. T'was certainly better than sittin' on your backside in some godforsaken hole in the desert with some Arab taking pot shots at you every time you went for a crap."

The captive stared bewilderedly at the Sergeant. He began to shiver.

"I'd polished my rifle and sharpened my bayonet, and I was eager for the off. After months of training, I was looking forward to gettin' my first real sight of the enemy. Needless to say, most of us never got close enough to see a thing."

The Sergeant paused for a moment and bowed his head as if in prayer.

"I was in charge of a group of fifteen men. Bairns really, most not even shaving. They were more enthusiastic than me and part of the problem was keeping them under control, reigning in that youthful exuberance. The whistle went, and up we climbed, and along we ran, shoutin', firin', roarin' with the sheer exhilaration of it all. I remember calling to the lads to keep in attacking pattern, but in the excitement they forgot their training and fanned out across the battleground. I looked across and saw them laughin' and cheerin' as they fired their rifles in to the darkness. For a few seconds it was the best time of my life."

"And then came the sound. The quick-fire rattle of the machine guns, clattering, like Death tapdancing on your coffin. I felt the whoosh of the bullets as they flew past my face and exploded in to the youngsters behind. One by one I saw their heads erupt in to a bloody mess. I saw limbs blown off, bodies ripped in half, innards splattered across a field the size of a footie pitch. I put my arm out to drag one of the younger lads to the ground, but by time he hit the mud his brain was dribbling down my shirt. Shells fell from the sky like - like fiery rain, pockin' and scorchin' the wet earth. The ground hissed as if life was escaping from the soil. And through the deaf'ning noise of the bombs and the bullets, I could still hear the screams of my men, high pitched wailing like a thousand demons cackling with laughter."

The Sergeant paused. His face was blank and his eyes focused on a point far behind the soldier. His mouth continued to open and close but no sound emerged, the brain unable to find words to describe the images replaying in his mind. For several minutes he continued to stare unblinking through the German and in to the past until he appeared to reach a part of his recollections of which he could speak.

"The guns stopped and the light from the explosions gradually faded away." He hesitated, "And then it turned dark." The Sergeant

42

closed his eyes and slowly shook his head as he struggled to picture a scene with no light. His eyes screwed up tightly, almost painfully, squinting for a memory. "Not a normal darkness. This was black, as black as tar and as heavy. It fell upon the field and straight away you could feel it stickin' to you, bending yer spine. It weighed on the maimed and the injured as they tried to crawl to their trenches and it crushed down on to the chests of the men gasping for breaths."

"There wasn't much shoutin', which was a surprise. Most just groaned in the dark. Some cried. There was no order to anything. Everyone was too busy dealing with their own personal agonies. I began to run but tripped over somethin' in the mud and just lay there. There was nae point. The darkness made you blind and the mud made you lame." His voice was faltering now as the images became too painful. "I lay there in the cold, mud freezing on my face, and looked up at the sky. I remember it was a sparkling night. Thousands of stars twinkling in the heavens. You could see the Milky Way cutting across the sky leaving a trail of diamonds. And I can remember thinkin', it was a beautiful night to die." He went silent for several minutes and then added bitterly. "And die we did. In the dark, in the cold, miles from home, pushed in to the mud by the weight of this beautiful night."

He clenched his fists as he struggled to stifle his sobbing.

"There was death everywhere," he continued in rapid breaths. "You couldn't see it but you could smell it alright. Cooked flesh. Fresh blood. It was slaughter. Nothin' could have lived through that. Not our soldiers, not our spirits. Nothing." The Sergeant was staring straight ahead now, tears frosted on his cheeks. "I reached out to see what'd tripped me. My hand hit some metal, icy to touch. A helmet or somethin'. And next to it, in the filth, somethin' soft."

He paused and looked down wide eyed at his hands, then continued at speed. "Just then flares suddenly lit up the sky overhead, blanking out the stars, and for the first time we saw the situation around us. And d'you know what? D'you what, my Krauty friend? Death wasn't all around, as I thought. No, there was life everywhere," his voice rising. "The ground, the ground itself, the rotten, stinkin', suckin' mud, it was alive. You see, it was moving. It was wrigglin' and wormy with my men." He began to shake. There were noises in the background. They were ignored. "I looked at my hands. They were all knarled and frozen with cold, puckered and wizened like a' old man's. And they were holding a face. A perfectly normal, perfectly formed, human face. A face, for the love of God." He began to weep uncontrollably. Across the field in another trench the moonlight caught the movement of something dark and shiny. The Sergeant looked up and roared. "A face that hours earlier had been laughin' and talkin' and smokin' and eating. It could have been anyone. Anyone of us. But now it was just a face, with not even a skull to make it smile."

He stood up and raised his pistol. The German's eyes widened in horror.

"This is for everything you took away".

The shot echoed in the still night. Darkness fell.

8.
THE STATION

At least it was dry in the station, Martin reasoned, as he struggled along the concourse angling himself forward against the squalling wind that blew in off the river. His coat was unbuttoned and it billowed in the gusts like a cape. Underneath, his clothes were still damp and the wind quickly whipped the moisture from the battered fibres of his shirt and jacket, and he began to shiver again.

He passed the huge electronic timetable without looking but felt sure that there would be a train for him somewhere. There were a few other people hanging around, mostly the drunk and the dispirited, but none seemed to be making for the trains. He wondered how many of them were like Tom and Victor, homeless except for the patch of ground on which they slept that night. Certainly no train stopped there, unless you counted the one which nightly unloaded humanity's cargo of misery and discomfort on the unfortunates of the city.

He had left his two new friends tucked up under the stairwell with their whisky a while ago. They had shared a glass or two and spent an easy time talking and laughing and swapping stories. Neither Tom nor Victor mentioned their past, nor how they had come to end up growing old in a rain soaked alleyway, and their tales were the same as those told around dinner tables the world over. Martin told them of Christopher and showed them a photo he kept in his wallet. They had both smiled and Tom put his hand on Martin's shoulder and gripped warmly. He did not mention his wife.

They spoke and joked for an hour or so and conversation flowed from Martin more readily than for many months. Time had passed quickly until a tired Tom reminded Martin that he had a warmer place to go to. Martin shook their hands with genuine affection and splashed through the grey puddles to the end of the alley where he stopped to wave. Tom and Victor were already asleep, bedded down for the night in cardboard and plastic and snuggled up in the grime. He hoped their dreams were as absent from the drudgery that filled their lives as was their conversation.

Martin now found himself at the very end of the platform having walked further than he'd planned. Looking up and down the platform he realised he was alone. The wind chaffed at his skin and he was cold and tired. He reached in to his pocket and pulled out his mobile phone. He ran his thumb over the crack in its face and then randomly pushed a few buttons, but nothing happened. His shoulders sagged. It was his third phone this year, which was, even for him, something of a record. It wasn't much of a problem, he decided. Chris would be in bed by now, and the train was already here, so he would be home within the hour.

The train was an old type, with a series of single compartments spreading the width of the carriage. Martin felt sure it was the right one. They always put the old carriages on the late run and judging by the absence of other commuters this must surely be the last train home for Christmas.

He clambered up into the carriage and was gratified by the warmth which greeted him. He lay his head against the back of the seat, nodded to the old man sitting opposite and fell soundly asleep.

9.
THE YOUNGSTER

The man gazed absently out over the quiet streets. From up here you could see forever, the guide had said. She was right, after a fashion. You could certainly see a long way, all the way in to the future in fact: redundant dockyards, boarded up factories, fields lying fallow and overgrown, and way down below, barely visible, lines of unemployed men sitting outside public houses downing their beer and sorrows.

They said it was a depression. How apt, he thought. But this was not the Great Depression, that had come and gone. This was the doing of one company, or to be more accurate, one person. Why it had happened, how it had happened, was not entirely clear to him, not even from up here. All he knew was that one moment he'd had a successful job and an outstanding future, and then everything had changed.

For a brief moment, the man closed his eyes, as if deep in thought. He appeared a sullen and somewhat dishevelled figure, despite the expensive cut of his clothes. The town below was bathed in the late afternoon sun, weak and watery, but he stood in the shade, at ease in the gloom. The light was dim here and the air cold with the bite of mid-winter, yet his jacket remained undone, his waistcoat unfastened. A brisk wind, sharp with the tang of the sea, blew in off the port and buffeted against his ageing frame. He remained unmoved and continued staring emptily down at the town from the shadows.

How had it come to this, he asked himself. He had worked so hard. They both had, him and the Youngster. The Youngster. The man forgot how young the lad was at times. He seemed to have built up a cold heartedness it would take most other men three times as long to accumulate. The tycoon and his apprentice they had called them, at first, taking the markets by storm and leading the way in the modernisation of a modernising world; upstarts from the provinces showing the big city players how to revamp and run a business in the new era. In the space of six years they had transformed the old company and turned their tacky and forgotten seaside town in to the centre of a commercial empire that stretched to the cities and beyond. Success had followed success as they had rapidly expanded from the early days of agriculture, initially in to manufacturing, and then, at the Youngster's urging, in to the world of finance. They invested heavily, not just in the company but also in the town and the people in it, with the result that the town's population doubled and living standards rose to levels unthinkable only a few short years before. The town became a boom town; a tourist boom followed a property boom which itself followed on from an employment boom.

And as the town grew famous, so did they. The perfect team, the unbeatable match of the old and new, mixing his wise and careful approach with the youthful daring of his fearless underling. They became the first of a new breed of celebrity businessmen with their faces regularly spread across the pages of the national newspapers, and everyone, from radio stations to magazine editors, merchant banks to politicians, clamouring for an audience. They were widely seen as encapsulating the mood of the time: wealthy philanthropic industrialists who not only provided the community with jobs but also with hospitals for the sick and hostels for the poor. The local population saw the company as a symbol of social and economic recovery from the grinding hopelessness of the Depression and they viewed the two men who were its driving force as torch bearers of a kinder world to come.

And the truly wonderful thing was that it worked. The workforce was happy and therefore productive, which meant the company's profits soared and the workers' wages rose, and everyone benefited. The company's motto became, "To Serve All", and this they did. He made it company policy to regularly donate to local charities and good causes, and with the company's financial clout they could entice over some of the big stars from the rapidly burgeoning film industry across the Atlantic. They had Fay Wray opening a new community centre and Johnny Weissmuller cutting the ribbon on a school which the company had rebuilt after it had become rotten with neglect. Many pupils from the school naturally looked to join the company on graduation. While Weissmuller was over, they also got him to open a new factory, which provided good publicity at a time when their rivals were threatening a takeover bid.

To commemorate their achievement they rebuilt the old clocktower in the middle of the high street and dedicated it to all the people who had worked to make the company and the town such a success. When the town's open-top trams circled the tower, the company guides would tell them that the red brick edifice, reconstructed after decades of dereliction and now standing tall against the easterly sea winds, was a vivid symbol of hope for the future and glory in achievements past. (The Youngster had hastily written those words for the programme on a piece of paper in between meetings, he was later to boast).

Yes, life had been good for the tycoon and his apprentice with the future seeming as comforting and sure as the springtime sun.

From his vantage point high above the town the man squinted at the brilliant red of the horizon and briefly sighed. He remembered the warm glow of success and how good it had felt after the cold, hard years of war and austerity. Hardened by the memory of the Depression, he'd been determined to enjoy it to the full and had decided that a rich and successful man like him should be able to spend more time with his growing family.

Weekends off became the rule and he even managed to spend a holiday together with his family for the first time in seven years. He remembered lying on a sun-drenched beach, a fresh sou'westerly cooling his reddened skin, watching his sons play football and feeling ashamed at how much they had grown unnoticed. He took to leaving home late so that the family could breakfast together and several evenings each week were put aside for barbeques by the pool. It was the happiest of times.

Inevitably such new demands on his time meant that he began to take his eye off the business, leaving progressively more in the hands of the Youngster who had no such homely distractions. Soon the apprentice was making key decisions in the senior man's absence and subtly altering the company's policies so that the business began to reflect his more contemporary views on efficiency and success.

The Youngster started slowly cutting back on all miscellaneous outgoings, expenditure not related directly to the company, including the majority of the business's charitable donations. These were considered non-revenue generating activities that wasted capital and bit in to the company's profitability and, importantly, in to the Youngster's own pocket. Unlike his boss, the Youngster did not accept the long term strategy, or simple humanity, of providing for a happy and secure workforce as an assured means of success. Productivity was not something to be teased from the workforce, the young man would proclaim, it was something to be demanded. If they were not productive, then the company would not pay for their services; other workers would be more than willing to step in to their shoes. The feelings and wellbeing of those the company employed were immaterial. They would find it a good sight unhappier without a job and on the streets.

And he, the father of the business, the fabled tycoon who had famously lost his fortune and then regained it in the space of five years, had nodded weakly and allowed it to happen, content to let the aggressive young man have his head while he wiled away the summer in the garden with his kids. Things would be fine, he had told himself. The lad would eventually see sense, would burn his fingers, get hurt, and learn a little human spirit. Anyway, the company had too good a name and too vast a financial reserve to be at any risk.

In the fading glow of sunset, the man shook his head at his naivety.

Statutes were changed on the company's books, legally but quietly, new appointments made without the senior partner's knowledge and influential contacts forged. Slowly and inexorably power passed from the tycoon to his apprentice, until in the winter of thirty-seven with the country in the grip of the great freeze and dark forces unfolding across the Continent, it became obvious that the student had become the master. The sound business acumen and kindly paternalistic approach of the older tycoon were replaced by the brash individualism of the Youngster.

Immediately the new boss set about paring down the workforce in a brutal attempt to streamline the business. Employees with long and unblemished records were sacked for trivial offences and subsidiary family firms who had stuck by the company during the worst period of the Depression were taken over and apart and sold off in pieces. Any vestiges of philanthropy not already removed from the company's charter were eradicated. The school that the company had opened and overseen three years earlier fell into a state of disrepair more desperate than the one from which it had been rescued. Local goodwill evaporated and the company's gates were regularly daubed with graffiti, its rusted iron railings bent and scored; security guards of dubious criminal heritage were eventually employed on commission to guard the entrance. Hollywood stars no longer came to bless community projects and the time of celebrity passed to one of infamy as the company's approach to business became as harsh and self centred as the budding young mogul controlling it.

The man looked out across the darkening townscape. The mellow colours of dusk were hardening in to night. In the shadows on the dockside two gulls fought noisily over the carcass of a dead fish. Perhaps it was just the times, he thought. A pervasive sense of self concern seemed to be the legacy of the Depression. Gone was the caring collectivism of the post war years and in its place was a new generation being fed a social diet of selfishness and confrontation. Muscular young men in black shirts had already marched through the city and were now stamping their mark across Europe. He shivered as he remembered the sound of broken glass being trampled underfoot by line upon marching line of young men staring skywards, singing, their chests puffed with a sense of destiny. It may be that the Youngster was just a child of circumstance, thought the man, a human echo of the timbre of the time.

Yet the Youngster was not a naturally bad person. There was no malice in his actions. There was an undoubted meanness of spirit, a lack of compassion for those less fortunate, but there was no nastiness or vindictiveness. Many of the business decisions he made were strictly necessary and he saw them through with an admirable sense of self belief and purpose. It was just that this was done with a complete lack of thought for anyone else.

Examples of his uncaring single-mindedness were legion: from the dependable supplier forced in to bankruptcy because the company had brought in another marginally cheaper but unknown source, to the loyal worker sacked without warning for a minor transgression despite nearing retirement and never having missed a day in forty years. All actions justifiable on business grounds and all motivated by nothing more sinister than profit, and all unburdened by any sense of humanity. Balancing the books of kindness and charity, the Youngster would say, was not his concern. He closed down entire factories because he thought them unprofitable and then opened them again a month or so later when the market had picked up and desperate workers would graft for less pay. Shipments of goods from abroad were turned back at the docks because cheaper sources had been uncovered closer to home. The ship would then be stranded in port with an unwanted cargo, leaving the seamen with no money to get home or eventually with food to eat. He would then make a bid way below the true value for the goods rotting in the boxes and the captain would have no choice but to accept. By that time some of the sailors had already been taken on by the company to work at menial rates, having been persuaded in a language they barely understood that their only chance of a passage home was with the regular work the company could offer. To be fair, several settled successfully and worked their way up the business to well paid and influential positions. Many more, however, never escaped the smell and sweat of the docks and spent their time soaked in rum staring in to the blackened waters of the port. Few ever made it home.

Yes, people called the Youngster heartless, and they were right, to an extent. He had feelings, but they were for himself. He was simply a young man who cared little for anyone else or their predicament.

The man knew little of his background. He had employed him as a teenager on the advice of a reliable business acquaintance who had spotted a drive and maturity way beyond the kid's years. He knew the lad was fatherless and had been raised initially by his young mother and then by his aunt when his mother had married a man of whom the Youngster loudly disapproved. Apparently he had refused to take the name of his new step-father and instead reverted to using his mother's maiden name just to emphasize his dissatisfaction. It was then they had moved to the town. The young man's aunt was a strongwilled woman, by all accounts, and a harsh disciplinarian who attempted to keep the headstrong boy out of trouble at a time when trouble was around every corner and in every home. Her apparent success said much for them both.

It cannot have been easy for the Youngster, the man reflected, growing up in a time of austerity with no father figure to look up to or learn from. The contrast between the man's carefree childhood full of climbing trees and throwing stones and of long summers and family picnics was stark. It was said that the Youngster carried an old faded photograph of his father in his wallet. If true, it was a singular demonstration of sentimentality from someone who was palpably uneasy with any form of affection and whose sole emotional high appeared to be pleasure at his own financial success.

The man recalled how he had invited the lad over for Christmas lunch two years ago, concerned that he was going to spend the holidays alone, and how the Youngster had doggedly tried to wriggle out of the invitation. He had only relented when it became obvious that his boss expected him to attend - the older man was in charge in those days. The Youngster had turned up early, visibly pale, and had sweat coldly with discomfort throughout the meal. The man had carved the turkey and the children had wished and his wife had fussed and everyone had cheered, but nothing could warm the poor lad or his mood. He talked politely when everyone else was shouting, he smiled with restraint when the whole family were bellylaughing; he even pulled the crackers with the kids in such an awkward manner that they consistently failed to pop and, indeed, struggled to even tear. The paper hat that little Millicent insisted the young man wear sat so reluctantly on his head it was as if it objected to crowning someone who found the festive spirit so obviously disquieting. Within minutes it had baled out and joined the steadily increasing pile of streamers and crepe paper on the floor. After lunch, when they all gathered in the living room to sit by the fire and open the presents from under the Christmas tree, the Youngster's unease became acute and he made his excuses and left, forgoing the offer of a lift home. He left behind his hat and coat and the gifts the family had bought for him. If truth be told, his wife was relieved; the atmosphere was becoming a little strained. Later on, when the family sat down for tea, the man wondered how the Youngster would spend the rest of the day. He loved the whole idea of Christmas and it was not a time of year that he liked to think of people sitting alone with their thoughts. Later that week he noticed the young man's signature in the company register for December the twenty-fifth, a tiny, heavy handed scrawl sitting alone at the top of a blank page.

However, despite his lack of social skills, the Youngster had never let his emotional incompetence hinder his progress in the company. In fact, by the time he came to buy his senior partner out, he had turned it from a social embarrassment in to one of the main driving forces behind his success; it left him unencumbered by the sensitivities with which more kindly souls were weighed down.

The buy-out was a good deal, too generous to refuse, the man's lawyers had assured him. Apart from the financial considerations, it was clear that his services were no longer essential to the well being of the company. It was still making money, a good deal of money, despite the fact that he, the founding father, had slipped quietly in to the backseat of the boardroom many months before. It was also plain that the Youngster would never again allow his older partner to drive the company he had built from scratch.

The deal involved a mixture of capital and assets: a sizeable chunk of cash together with stock representing a twenty percent stake in one of the smaller firms controlled by the company.

The man spent the money with unbridled glee. Whatever wealth he had acquired up till then had been either tied up in some form of business venture or reinvested in to the company. His house was heavily mortgaged and most of his other possessions were acquired by some sort of loan system the company's accountants had devised and which was utterly alien to him. But now he had money, real money, notes that he could see and feel and spend.

He took to taking out large sums of cash from the bank and then walking in to upmarket shops and buying whatever took his fancy. The feel of his thick wallet resting comfortingly against his thigh was his reward for a lifetime of toil, he told himself. His wife objected, pleaded caution, but he had worked hard for these hedonistic pleasures, he deserved it.

Seven months later the money had almost gone. Hangers-on and the giddy addiction of his new found spending power had eaten swiftly in to his fortune. In an effort to claw some money back, the man invested what was left and all that he could borrow from the bank in to several ailing companies which his inside contacts had assured him were due to rise rapidly in value. But the months of easy living had blunted his business mind and the companies' worth continued to fall until he was forced to sell at a tremendous loss to the very people who had advised him to buy in the first place. In the new world, friends and money did not mix, the old world tycoon was beginning to understand.

The Youngster had watched all this with a detached interest and was able to guess his former partner's next move. Knowing that he would be compelled to sell the stock he had been given as part of his farewell package, the Youngster gave instructions to sell the company's controlling interest in the same firm to a little known associate outside the business.

As expected, the next few days saw the firm's value fall dramatically with the inevitable uncertainty generated by the withdrawal of a major financial player. The Youngster then had someone buy his former partner's stock at the new vastly deflated price, together with the re-purchase of the associate's stock, and sat back and watched with mild contentment as confidence returned, stocks rose and the company made a tidy profit, a tenth of which would eventually wend its way in to the Youngster's annual bonus. He did not consider the twenty-three people at the firm who had lost their jobs a as result of the chaos.

The man was distraught. The price he had got for the stocks was not enough to cover his debts. In order to keep his predicament from his wife and to spare the kids any suffering, he managed to borrow some more money from several obscure financial institutions, and when these debts were called in, he borrowed still more from unknowing friends.

In desperation he went to see his former apprentice, and friend, to ask for a loan. The Youngster listened attentively and with apparent sympathy to his story, and then, in the matter-of-fact way of a newsreader reporting a national tragedy, pointed out that his situation was entirely of his own making and that the company could not afford to bale out all those former employees who had got themselves in to financial trouble. Having pulled the company through the Depression he should be aware of that more than anyone, he added in the same detached tone.

After this, the man's circumstances began to spiral rapidly downwards. He tried other places for money, but word had spread amongst his former associates in the business world and suddenly calls went unreturned and doors remained closed. Life at home began to suffer as he fought to keep the secret of his shame from his family. He began to argue with his wife over trivial things and on one unforgivable day he slapped his son for being insolent. That night was spent in a seedy hotel staring at the ceiling and quivering with self loathing. He could not believe that a life of hard work had led to this. The debts rapidly mounted and the dogs began to close in, until one day, his mind fractured by despair, he realised that the wonders of modern insurance meant he was worth more to his family dead than alive.

The tower clock struck ten. It was time for his Christmas present.

Yes, from up here you could see forever, but it was dark now and forever did not seem as far. He jumped.

As the ambulances arrived and the police began to ask questions and to assemble details of the jumper's life, a train was pulling out of the town's main station. A young man, dressed older than his years, was running determinedly for it. It was the last one home for Christmas and although he would have preferred to work a little later, he had resolved to treat himself to a day off this year. He had promised his aunt he would be there for Christmas lunch; he would not, of course, but he would pop in some time in the evening. He owed the old bat that much.

The train gathered speed and began to pull away from him. He was not going to make it. He would have to get a taxi, after all. Silently he damned the unnecessary expense. As his legs began to slow and the train began to quicken, an old man reached out from one of the carriages, grabbed him by the arm and with a laugh that could be heard above the rushing wheels, pulled him on to the train with uncommon strength.

10.
MR STANLEY BARWELL

"Thanks very much," gasped the Youngster. "Didn't think I'd make it," he added, panting heavily, the flushed cheeks of his pinched face inflating and deflating with asthmatic rapidity.

The old man nodded his head and smiled benignly.

The train picked up speed and the Youngster stretched out his arm to balance himself. It was sore. The old chap must have given it quite a yank, he thought. He was strong for someone his age.

The Youngster waited until the train had steadied and his breathing slowed and then made to sit down.

"Excuse me," he huffed pushing past the splayed legs of the man sleeping in the corner of the carriage. Martin did not stir.

He heaved his briefcase on to the overhead rack and removed his hat and coat. He was not in the best of shape, especially in view of his young age, and a small belly pushed tightly against the belt of his thick, worsley trousers. A thin film of perspiration was seeping in to his undershirt and it clung uncomfortably to his back. A working lifetime of sitting at desks meant that the sprint for the train was probably one of the few major physical exertions he had indulged in since school, even though childhood was a time he remembered as empty of much of the play that seemed to lighten other boys' journeys from infancy to adolescence. He loosened his tie, flapped the inside of his shirt collar in an effort to release the hot sticky air trapped inside and sat down opposite the old man, and tried to settle.

Several minutes later, he was still inexplicably twitchy and restless. Try as he might, he could not get comfortable. The seat was too lumpy, the carriage too hot, and, what's more, he could feel the old man staring at him from across the compartment. The Youngster knew what was expected of him, but the thought of two strangers with nothing in common being obliged to indulge in meaningless conversation simply because of their chance proximity to each other ... he struggled to imagine anything more pointless. It was one of the reasons he hated trains; people were always trying to talk to him.

The two men sat in strained silence for several minutes. The dull rhythm of the train accentuated the quiet. The Youngster tried to read his newspaper, but it rustled in time with the wheels of the train, so he folded it neatly in to quarters and lay it across his lap. It felt suffocatingly warm in the carriage. Several times he ran his fidgety hand sideways across his scalp, smoothing his short, heavily-greased hair flat on to his head. A bead of sweat edged along the ridge of his eyebrow until a momentary juddering of the carriage interrupted the train's soporific rumble and shook the droplet to his cheek. He lifted his head to wipe it with the sleeve of his jacket and caught the old man's stare.

"Thought I'd have to get a wretched taxi," the Youngster conceded.

There was no response.

"If I could find one on such an awful night," he continued.

The old man said nothing.

After several seconds the Youngster looked back down at his paper and pretended to read, reflecting on the fact that idle conversation was even more uncomfortable than he remembered. The businessman in him momentarily wondered why people indulged so readily in such a vacuous exercise. It didn't make sense; it was costly in time, yet completely worthless. ('Nothing earned, Nothing gained' was the company's maxim, and the Youngster was nothing if not a company man.) More importantly, it also demanded a degree of social skill and a familiarity with human nature which he had yet to acquire, and as such, it unnerved him beyond all reason.

"How far were you planning to go?" the old man asked eventually, his voice deep and strong.

"Marsden."

The small village was about ten miles along the coast.

"Saved yourself," the old man stated.

"Yes, I'm sure a taxi would have cost a well-earned shilling or two."

"Would have cost a great deal."

A quizzical look flitted across the Youngster's face.

"Are you from around here?" he asked, soldiering on.

"No." The Youngster took in the old man's dark skin and worn, fur-lined coat. "And yes."

"Oh, I see," lied the Youngster. "Do - do you have family in the area?" he tried.

"No immediate relations," replied the old man slowly. "Although I have family everywhere." The Youngster nodded vacantly. "You may say, I work in these parts," added the old man.

He was a little old to still be working, thought the Youngster. But these were hard times and he was a deceptively powerful fellow. Unthinkingly, he rubbed his arm.

"Whereabouts?"

"Here and there."

"Ah-ah," acknowledged the Youngster, now thoroughly disconcerted. A few moments of confused silence followed until the Youngster piped in desperation, "Still, at least it's stopped raining," and turned his head to look out the window at the darkness.

The conversation stopped. The encounter had left the Youngster a little flustered, an emotion to which he was unaccustomed and which he suffered with a degree of disquiet. He felt that in the currency of words he had paid sufficiently for the old man's help and, in any case, the banter was hardly flowing. The old man's truncated and ambiguous answers jutted in to the conversation, checking its course, like buttresses along an ancient river.

"Did you mean the weather?" asked the old man suddenly.

"I'm sorry?"

"When you said it was an awful night, did you mean the weather?" He paused. "Or were you referring to the nature of the day?"

The Youngster squinted with the effort of understanding.

"Christmas Eve," helped the old man.

"Oh!" exclaimed the Youngster, marginally less confused. "The, er, the weather, I suppose," he stumbled. After a moment's introspection he repeated, "Yes, the weather," assuring himself.

The old man nodded but said nothing.

The Youngster turned back to the window. It was going to be a long journey, he thought. Next time, it would have to be a taxi. Damn the expense.

The minutes passed slowly. The Youngster tried to occupy himself - he had, after all, a good deal of work to do before he could retire tonight - but he was finding it unusually difficult to concentrate. However hard he tried, his thoughts seemed to be constantly and irresistibly drawn back to the strange old man sitting opposite. It was a distraction that was both troubling and time consuming.

He could see him now in the dim reflection of the carriage window, sitting, half-smiling to himself, his head titled to one side as if listening to an inner voice, or a quiet whisper from far away. One hand played in his big bush of a beard and the other lay across his corpulent middle, now and again tapping the rhythm of the wheels on his midriff. Whatever world his mind inhabited, he was happy there.

The Youngster was desperate not to get drawn in to another conversational puzzle and so he sat rigidly looking out of the window, concentrating all his efforts on staring past the old man's reflection and in to the night. It was like staring through a ghost.

It was dark outside. Very dark, in fact. Actually, he really could not see much at all. He cupped his hands around the centre of the glass to block out the carriage lights and peered out through the clear black portal. Still he could see nothing. The rain had stopped and the clouds had cleared, but there was not a glimmer of life or living. He breathed on to the glass and rubbed feverishly until a large circle appeared in the window grime and a thick black mark stained the cuff of his shirt. Nothing.

He knew they were now travelling through mainly agricultural land, he knew because he owned most of it, but he would have expected to see the lights of the farmhouses and of the little rows of tied cottages which the company had bought off the landowners. He was sure of their position because he remembered the fuss that had been created by their purchase. The company's lawyers had had to work day and night to fight off a rival bid by a co-operative representing the families who had lived in the cottages for generations. Even when the deal was closed some of the co-op's members picketed the cottages and prevented access for a month or so. It was a futile gesture, thought the Youngster, the company was never going to change its mind and, whatever their strength of purpose, people will always succumb to hunger and cold if left long enough. It was one the earliest lessons he had learnt as company chairman.

The cottages were presently occupied by some of the company's security guards, if his memory served him correctly, and it usually did. They were let to the guards on a temporary basis until the company decided what to do with the pretty flint buildings.

But he could see no sign of any of this. It was a cold night, surely the guards and their families would have fires lit and hot drinks on the stove ? At the very least there should be a smudge of light from the steamed up windows of the tavern.

"Looking for something?" asked the old man

The Youngster turned in surprise.

"No, not really," he responded rather timidly. The Youngster had momentarily forgotten the old man's presence and his sudden interjection had caught him off guard. "No nothing at all," he added in stronger tones.

"You seem to be peering out in a rather," the old man hesitated for a moment, "tenacious manner."

"Simply trying to spot a few things," replied the Youngster curtly.

"And did you?"

"Did I what?" His words had an edge.

"Did you find what you were looking for?"

"No," snapped the Youngster. "No I did not, if you must know."

"I see."

The Youngster realised that he had been brusque with the old man. This was hardly new. It was something at which he was well practised; indeed, he had honed abruptness in to a formidable negotiating skill. What was new, however, was that it bothered him. It was only a niggling awareness, but it scratched at his conscience.

"I was trying to find out where we were," he relented. "I thought I knew, but I could not see the lights of the village, so I must have been mistaken." He thought for a moment. "Although I still would have expected to see something."

"I see," repeated the old man.

"Where is everybody?" muttered the Youngster. "The moon is full and it's a clear night."

"Perhaps the night is not as clear as you think."

"Perhaps not."

The train rumbled on through the darkness.

"I'm cold," said the tall, grey-looking man sitting across the carriage.

The Youngster had not noticed him before. He had a narrow, angular face and sported a thin moustache that only exaggerated his drawn features. His skin had a mottled, unhealthy pallor and a dull sheen which reflected the lights of the carriage. Even from where the Youngster was sitting he could see that the glaze of the man's skin was not a warm shine, not the comforting glow of exertion or over-indulgence. He had seen it many times before as a child, he noted with distaste. It was the buff, cold, clammy reflection of poverty.

"I'm cold," the tall man repeated, more slurred this time.

He was asleep and obviously dreaming, albeit noisily. His eyes opened for an instant and stared, unseeing. They were set in deep hollows, like black craters on an ashen moonscape.

"Cold," he mumbled softly and then seemed to settle. A thin rivulet of saliva dribbled from the corner of his mouth.

It was still hot in the carriage and the sleeping man was wrapped in a thick jacket that was frayed and muddied.

"Cold?!" tutted the Youngster, shaking his head. Instinctively he looked across at the old man and lifted his eyes to the ceiling acknowledging the mutual embarrassment of sharing the compartment with such a delirious individual.

Without a word the old man removed his coat and placed it across the sleeping man's broad, bony shoulders. The Youngster looked at him incredulously.

"Do you know him?" he asked.

"No more than I know you."

"But..." stuttered the Youngster.

"Is there a problem?"

"Well, he does not look terribly clean," said the Youngster nodding to the man's unshaven face and grimy hands. "He's probably drunk, judging by look of him. Or mad."

The old man said nothing but there was a hint of disapproval in his expression.

"Or diseased," added the Youngster. He was beginning to feel a now familiar sense of disquiet. "He may have a contagion or some kind of infestation," he tried.

"I do not believe so."

"You know nothing about him."

"I know that he is cold."

"And that's all that matters?"

"What else would you have me consider?"

The Youngster was momentarily lost for an answer.

"If I said that I was cold, would you give me your coat?" he mustered.

"I do not think my coat would provide the warmth you need, my friend," replied the old man softly.

The Youngster knew he had lost the point, but his pride refused to let the matter rest. The old man may have been proving rather more lucid than at first, but the last word was a luxury to which he had grown accustomed.

"It may have been generous of you, but, I maintain it was rather unwise," he muttered and looked down at his folded hands, as if bringing the conversation to an end.

"How can generosity ever be unwise?" persisted the old man.

The Youngster looked up, his instincts sensing safer ground. "Show me a generous man, and I will show you a poor man."

"Surely you do not believe that?"

"I do so, sir, and more."

"I find it hard to take your words seriously, all the more so because of the time of year," the old man said. His tone was sombre.

"Well you should, sir," replied the Youngster, enthused. The reference to the time of year passed unnoticed. "I am a business man, a successful business man, and I have made my fortune understanding people and what drives them." The Youngster was now in full flight. "And I assure you that a generous nature, while perhaps of laudable intention, disadvantages both the giver and the receiver."

"I cannot subscribe to such a view," said the old man dismissively. "Especially on this day of all days."

"It is true nonetheless," he responded, "irrespective of the day or the time. Charity and munificence pick at a man's pocket and produce citizens dependent on handouts rather than their own travails. It depresses the urgency for hard work and kills the spirit."

"More so than cold or misery or hunger?"

"There is nothing like an empty stomach for igniting the need for labour. Believe me, I know of which I speak."

"I believe you have experience in these matters."

The Youngster paused.

"Do you know who I am?" he asked, his eyes shining.

"Should I?"

"Yes sir, you should. I am Mr Stanley Barwell". At the absence of recognition he added, "Chairman of Torwell Industries,"

"Stanley who?" the man enquired.

"Barwell. Stanley Barwell," urged the Youngster, his face reddening. "My company owns most of the land through which we are now travelling. It also owns the town and docks where I boarded the train and most of the surrounding countryside, or at least the parts of it which are profitable."

The old man inflated his capacious chest and let out a long low whistle.

Undaunted, the Youngster continued, "And I gained that success by understanding business and people's places within it. You have to know what makes the workers work," he declared, pointing to his head, visibly smug at his alliterative turn of phrase.

"Am I to assume that you consider yourself something of an expert in this field?" asked the old man. The unhurried and melodic rhythm of his voice buffeted the force of the Youngster's speech.

"You assume correctly," he replied, his momentum suddenly checked. "Ask the people of Wallingtom."

"Wallingtom?"

"Yes, Wallingtom," repeated the Youngster, mildly annoyed. "The company town? The economic miracle of the thirties? It is a famous story."

"I am sorry. I have been busy with other stories," responded the old man.

A questioning look skimmed the Youngster's face and his argument slowed once more. He inhaled deeply.

"Wallingtom is what it is today because of my hard work," he declared. "I saved it from the run down, decaying fishing village it had become after the war and gave it back a life."

"That's very noble of you. I hope the townspeople appreciate what you have done for them."

"I would hope they do. Without me there would be no jobs, no houses, no food and no future."

"In that order?"

"In whatever order," he growled. "The company is their provider."

"Would it not be kinder for them to provide for themselves?"

"Meaning what?" The Youngster was taken aback. He was not used to being questioned on company matters.

"It seems to me that for a man to be so beholden to a corporation that he relies on it for the necessities of everyday life, for the food on the table, the roof overhead, then he condemns himself to a life spent fearing the day when the corporation is no longer there to provide."

The Youngster's eyes lit up.

"Without knowing it, sir, you have hit upon the founding principle of many a successful business in this day and age. People will only work at their most efficient if they know their position is not assured. They need to feel the desperate breaths on their necks of the hungry workers waiting in the wings, men who will sweat more for less pay. Any suggestion that the company is a generous employer - forgiving transgressions, caving to wage demands, dolling out bonuses, paying for sickness and idleness and the like - will be taken to mean that the company is a weak employer and that the workers need not work hard to keep their job. Security breeds complacency which begets laziness. Profits are not built on laziness. Keep the workers sharp, and keep the profits high, that's what I say."

The old man frowned.

"And you ask me when is generosity unwise," smirked the Youngster, shaking his head.

"I am afraid to say I remain unconvinced."

The Youngster swelled with incredulity. His argument had been powerful and coherent and the salient points forcibly made; it was unthinkable that the old man had been left untouched by his assertions. Deliberately, he looked the old man up and down.

"You are a generous man," he sighed, as if drawing the discussion to its inevitable but reluctant conclusion, "but as a generous man, if you'll forgive me, you will always be a poor man."

The old man glanced down at his well-worn clothes and at the tall man now sleeping quietly across the carriage.

"Yes, I expect you can afford many coats."

"I have a wardrobe full," boasted the Youngster.

"It is a pity then that you may only ever wear one." The old man paused. "Whereas a generous man may be cloaked in the gratitude of many. Who is the richer?"

The Youngster stuttered, and the train shuddered to a halt. Without looking at each other, the old man and Mr Stanley Barwell, esteemed Chairman of Torwell Industries, disembarked, the train's shrill whistle scraping across the taut silence.

As the pair walked alone along the platform bound in a freezing, swirling fog, there was a faint noise on the breeze. Some said it sounded like an old man laughing.

THE LAST TRAIN HOME

11.
THE YOUNG BOY AND JESSICA

"Can you spare some change, please. Just some coins for a cup of tea." The voice crackled in the chill night air. "A little cup of Christmas cheer?"

The young boy squatting outside the station waiting room was hard to see at first, but as Barwell and the old man approached the fog drifted clear and revealed him on his haunches wrapped in a tartan blanket, palm covered in an old woollen glove and outstretched.

"A little change for some tea, gents?" the boy piped on seeing the two men emerging from the mist. "To keep us warm," he implored, shivering rather dramatically.

The old man stopped and smiled at the boy.

"Something to take the chill from the bones. Not much. Just a cuppa tea." The boy gazed up at the old man, his eyes wide and beseeching. It was the over-pleading look of someone with a degree of experience in these matters. "Or two," he added.

Barwell slowed his walking and glanced briefly at the young wretch. A look of unease played across his face and he quickly turned away. He made to walk on.

"Where are you going?" asked the old man. His tone was soft but firm.

"Home," replied Barwell, taken aback. "Although I don't see what concern it is..."

"Are you not going to give the boy something?"

The young lad was still looking upwards, holding his position. Without losing his pained expression, he subtly nodded his head in agreement with the old man and turned his eyes to Barwell.

"Why?" asked Barwell.

The boy's brow furrowed slightly and he looked to the old man.

"It is cold and he is poor."

The boy nodded and turned to Barwell.

"Many are cold and poor."

He frowned and turned back.

"And it is Christmas."

A thin smile broached the boy's his imploring visage.

"And many have no-one to blame but themselves."

At the edges of the boy's overtly sad countenance a new emotion, exasperation, twitched at his face.

The old man looked aghast at Barwell and then down at the boy's painfully thin face.

"How old are you son?" he asked.

The boy's expression was now somewhat confused, but he remained staring upwards with his palm open.

"How old?" the boy repeated.

"Yes, how old."

"You're not from the Parish, are you?"

"No."

"Honest?"

"Cross my heart."

"Didn't think so. Dressed wrongly. Twelve, sir."

The old man heaved a sigh.

"I may be young but I still need to eat," reminded the boy, urging his palm upwards.

Reaching in to his jacket, the old man took out a few coins and placed them in the boy's hand. The young lad looked down at the coins, momentarily widened his eyes, then hurriedly palmed them in to the secret recesses of his blanket.

The old man turned to Barwell. "Twelve years old and the world is already blaming him, eh?!"

Barwell did not reply, but simply shuffled his feet awkwardly on the platform, clearly desperate to be elsewhere. Despite his disquiet, he felt his eyes drawn irresistibly to the young beggar. A small lamp hung from the waiting room porch and shone feebly through the fog down on to the crouching figure. It bathed the boy in a spray of watery yellow light that accentuated the bones of his face and cast long deep shadows under his eyes and cheekbones, making him appear hung and jaundiced. The blanket which wrapped around him like a shawl was matted and threadbare, but as the label indicated, it had seen better days. Barwell imagined it laid out with a sumptuous picnic on a summer's day surrounded by youngsters in white lace, munching and laughing. It was an incongruous image, certainly not from his childhood. Next to the wretch was a large bundle of rags and clothes together with a collection of what looked like old rugs and pieces of carpet; so much meaningless junk, thought Barwell. The boy was squatting with his back pressed against the glass door of the waiting room which was padlocked and bolted by several pieces of solid ironmongery. Inside, Barwell could make out a gas fire burning fiercely.

"Why is the room locked?" asked the old man.

"To keep us out, I s'pose. They think we'll take advantage. Still, the door's nice an' warm."

The inside of the glass was dripping with condensation as the warm air of the empty waiting room was cooled by the night. The old man looked up and down the empty, wet platform.

"You shouldn't be out here on your own on a night like this, son."

"I'm not alone, Jess is here somewhere. She's too young to do the late one, though. Not safe."

"Where are your parents?"

The young boy tipped back his head and laughed, and Barwell could see for the first time the sores around his mouth and the ulcers on his tongue. He also saw that the jaundice was not simply a trick of the light. He could look no more. The whole situation was beginning to sicken him.

"Are you okay?" the old man asked on seeing Barwell's discomfiture.

"I - I need to go. I have to leave." He was trembling. "Now," he added urgently.

"What's wrong?"

"Nothing. I'm just not very good in these situations. It always affects me like this."

"What does?" The old man could see Barwell was sweating.

"All this," swallowed Barwell, roughly pointing around him.

"I'm sorry, all this what?" asked the old man.

Barwell's gaze settled briefly on the boy. "Poverty," he whispered, through rapid breaths.

"Here you are, son," said Martin kindly, suddenly appearing out of the fog and throwing a couple of pounds in to the young boy's hand.

"How about me?" yawned Jessica emerging sleepily from under the pile of rugs and carpet.

Martin gave her some coins with a smile and before he could consider how young they both were, the boy tugged his sister up and they both scampered off in to the fog, leaving the warmth of the waiting room door behind.

"Merry Christmas," shouted the boy.

"Merry Christmas," his sister repeated.

The sound of their young voices was cushioned by the freezing fog, but their words hung in the air and sank slowly on to Barwell and Martin on the cold, damp mist.

"Christmas!" Barwell tutted to himself.

"Christmas," swallowed Martin. A sad smile stretched across his face.

The fog closed in again.

The young boy and Jessica stopped in a disused shed a few hundred yards from the station. They often used this place, mainly because it still had three of its walls standing and so was one of the warmest places around. It also had a light and the young boy reached up excitedly and turned it on.

He delved in to his tartan shawl and pulled out the unfamiliar coins Martin had given him; he put these respectfully to one side. Reaching further in to the ragged cloth, he retrieved the old man's coins and held them in his palm for inspection. Jessica screeched with excitement. The young boy simply smiled to himself, turned off the light and lay back on the hard ground, warmed by the thought that this was going to be a very special Christmas and definitely the last they would spend on the cold floor of a dilapidated outbuilding.

He closed his eyes and was soon lost in dreams of coal fires and soft beds and home. His hand was tightly clenched around the coins, but through the holes in his tattered glove shone a brilliant light, and when his dreams made his sleep restless and caused him to turn, a fine dust which sparkled in the moonlight cascaded through his fingers.

12.
BURYING DREAMS

Far out in the cold grey mist that hung over no-man's land crouched the Sergeant hacking at the frozen ground. He was digging a hole. He'd been scraping away for several hours now, but had made little impression on the solid earth.

Blood trickled down his arms. Holding his hands up to the steely sky, he saw that despite the chill air the blood was running freely in narrow rivulets from the nail beds of each finger. He spread his fingers and watched as the thin red lines, like the delta of a ruddy fertile river, merged together on the back of his hand to form a thick crimson stream which flowed down his arm and stained the cuffs of his khaki shirt.

Each fingernail was broken and jagged, but packed underneath the remaining shards was the bloody frozen topsoil of the killing grounds of war. Something told him that his fingers should hurt, but he felt no pain. Perhaps the cold had made them numb. They were not very effective in their present state, he knew. He could certainly do with a pick, or a shovel, or a knife, but none seemed to be around; and so, with a sigh, he continued as best he could, on his knees, scraping away at the iron ground.

Suddenly his fingers struck metal. It was a small star shaped object, a medal of sorts. As he brushed the flakes of earth from his icy find he was consumed by a sadness that this was all that was left of its owner's existence, the only proof that this man had lived and fought and died. It was a legacy made sadder by its commonality. Even now, far away, they were minting similar medals and fat men were sitting in warm factories stamping "The Front Line" on crates ready for shipment. Soon more shiny stars would become the sole record of other men's heroics. He felt an overpowering urge to bury it once more, but he knew he could not. He had to keep on digging until the grave had been dug. It was the least he could do.

The Sergeant awoke with a shudder. He was cold and disorientated, and shook at the memory of his dream, the last vivid images of which were still playing in his mind. The lights of the carriage were incomprehensible and painful at first, but they soon hastened his passage, blinking rapidly, from that dark fertility of half-sleep to the brighter, safer world of wakefulness. And as the brash lights came in to focus, they washed out the colours of his dream until they faded in to obscurity.

He had certainly slept the sleep of the dead. In fact, he could not remember having slept so deeply since he'd first moved to the Front. That meant he needed it, he told to himself. His body felt chilled, as if he had not moved all through his sleeping. Another sign that he needed it. Once, he had watched a young captain sleep seven straight hours sitting upright on a chair without moving a muscle, or dropping his playing cards. He had needed it too. He was killed the next day.

The Sergeant looked out of the window at the dense fog still swirling around the station. They won't be going anywhere until this clears, he said to no-one. He should settle down and get some rest. The dim memory of his dream made the thought of further sleep a little forbidding and so he decided to simply lie out and rest his aching limbs, but to avoid any further dozing. He pulled the old man's coat over his body and within minutes was snoring loudly. His gaunt cheeks were noticeably redder than before and he turned frequently without waking. After a short while all movement stopped except for his eyes which rapidly flicked from side to side, as if frantically trying to escape the darkness within. He was dreaming again.

13.
THE CHRISTMAS PARTY

"We're lost. I don't believe it, we're lost," complained Barwell stamping his feet on the damp cobbles like a truculent child.

"Are we?" asked the old man.

"Of course, we are. This damn fog has made us completely lose our way. It would not surprise me if we'd got off the train in the wrong place."

They had been walking for over thirty minutes, during which time Barwell had grown progressively more agitated, and cold. He now appeared to feel the need to impose his will on the group.

"What do you think?" Barwell asked Martin who seemed unbothered by the fuss.

"Well, it's certainly not Hanson Green," he shrugged.

"Where?"

"Hanson Green."

Barwell scowled. "No, it's not," he said, plainly annoyed. "And it's not Marsden, either."

"Never heard of it," replied Martin, unconcerned.

"Oh, this is no good. We'll have to knock on a house and ask directions."

"How about here?" The old man's deep voice brushed effortlessly through the fog, as if carried on a warm wind.

They looked up at the house. Its front was covered in white lights and the moist air split each one in to a spectacular starburst.

Barwell frowned.

"No, not here," he said quietly.

"Why not?" asked the old man.

"I don't think I'll be welcome here."

"Nonsense," said the old man. "It's Christmas Eve, I'm sure everyone will be welcome."

The party was in full swing and it took some time for their knocking to be answered. Finally, a lady - a guest, a maid, the host, it was difficult to tell, so little did she linger - opened the door and ushered them in with a broad smile and warm wishes for the season, and made it clear that, whatever their business, they were to enjoy themselves to the full. Then she whisked herself off in the direction of the ballroom leaving the three lost men warming quickly, if a little self consciously, in the hallway.

The whole house was decorated so beautifully and in such a festive manner that the mood of the men was uplifted simply upon entering. The old man roared his approval on seeing the glittering decor and slapped Barwell and Martin on the back with a hearty swing of his thick hands. The two men turned and stared at him.

"Oops," he mumbled. "Ehm, sorry," he added and then quickly wandered off to join the party, clearly struggling to maintain a po-face. A tinge of scarlet brushed his cheeks.

Barwell watched him go, rigid with shock. Martin simply shrugged and strolled off to get a drink, leaving Barwell alone in the hallway gazing with disquiet at the sumptuous decorations.

Behind him, new guests were arriving. The party was clearly a big occasion and the house thronged with people, most in dinner jackets or suits, but some in more relaxed dress. Whatever their attire, they all stopped in the hallway and marvelled at the decor. It was magnificently festive. The walls were green with holly, its bright red berries almost luminescent in the lights of the huge Christmas lanterns that hung from the ceiling; multicoloured balloons tied with multicoloured streamers danced on the warm air of the thick, red candles which stood on every sideboard and mantelpiece; tinsel twisted round the trunks of the massive oak beams of the ballroom like magical silver creepers, and in the hallway it weaved through the arms of the great chandelier so that when the ceiling shimmered in concert with the merrymaking far below, the crystal twinkled like an enormous star; miniature bells, tied with ivy and dusted with glitter, dangled from each doorway and tinkled cheerily whenever the guests danced through; there were baubles everywhere sparkling in the candlelight, and where they were not, there were ribbons, and where there were no ribbons there was mistletoe.

And the food! And the drink! The entire dining room was given over to a Yuletide feast of gargantuan proportions. There were hog roasts and jugged hares, game pies and roast partridges, and great swollen geese skewered through with a blackened spar and turning slowly over the fire hearth; those nearby were forced to hop repeatedly for cover as the birds' dripped fat on to the flames below and the fire spat out their pungent, lusty smell. Thick-legged turkeys were being cooled ready for carving beside succulent ducklings basted in their juices and steaming still. Laid out next to them and watched over by several sturdy chefs in starched white uniforms were a brace each of pheasants, woodcocks and pigeons, all cooked so their skin was crisp and brown but the meat still tender. Piles of roast potatoes, perfectly done, towered over a platter of vegetables three tables long. There were orange carrots and green beans and yellow swede and white parsnips and red cabbage, and smaller servings of all manner of more exotic vegetables such as pumpkin, squash and sweet potato. And in the middle of them all stood four enormous silver serving bowls etched with fine filigree and filled with bread sauce, cranberries, English mustard and thick brown gravy. On yet another table, this one circular, was an array of pears and apples, their skin as polished and smooth as pebbles in a stream, and fresh oranges, bananas and dark grapes glazed with icing sugar. Interspersed between them, as if gathered in for the winter, were bags of chestnuts and hazelnuts.

The old man looked wide-eyed upon the feast. He breathed deeply on the smell of the hot punch and mulled wine steaming in great copper bowls at the end of the food table and instinctively rubbed his throat made dry from the cold outside. A small, panicky looking gentleman, dressed in black tails and breeches, and visibly perspiring, was busy ladling out huge glasses of the red and burgundy-coloured drinks in to an unending line of small jugs held expectantly in front of him by the party guests. The man was doing his best to keep up with demand but the thirst of the guests was beginning to overwhelm him. He obviously took great pride in his work but was becoming increasingly red faced as his hands became a blur of ladling and pouring. Just as chaos appeared inevitable, help arrived in the shape of two young ladies, resplendent in blue and white frills, who with broad smiles and wide trays walked amongst the crowd refilling their glasses. The mass soon dwindled to a more manageable size, and to his considerable relief, the man was once more in control of his small corner of the room.

The old man chuckled to himself as the gentleman took his glass and, despite a brief and uncharacteristic hesitance, filled it expertly to the brim.

Martin looked around with a genuine smile on his face. He had not seen anything like this in years. The house practically tingled with seasonal spirit, and as he gaped in wonderment at it all, so his mind wandered, unburdened, and a host of childhood memories came rushing back.

He recalled the almost unbearable excitement of past Christmas Eves, of lying awake with his brother tortured by the knowledge that the next time they awoke it would be Christmas Day. He could remember vividly staring at the empty stocking at the foot of his bed and wrestling with the terrible problem of wanting to sleep, having to sleep, but being thoroughly unable to do so. And then, seemingly moments later, opening his eyes to see his stocking bulging with the marvellously irregular shapes of his Christmas presents. It was a truly magical sight, even in the dull wintry light of early morning. But even that was okay, because mum and dad would come in, bleary-eyed, and turn on the light and everything would be bathed in the orange brilliance of the bare sixty watt bulb which hung from the rough tiled ceiling.

There was something special about that light on Christmas morning. Throughout the year it was nothing more than a dull accompaniment to getting up for school, or to going to bed too early, or of frost on the windows, or of the musky smell of extra blankets. But on Christmas morning it was nothing short of a beacon signalling the start of the celebrations.

He found himself staring up at the ceiling glittering with angels and snowmen, half expecting a train of reindeer to come flying overhead. He laughed to himself. It was like a fairyland, this place, and was enough to bring out the child in anyone. The house reminded him of the grotto in that big city department store where they had taken Christopher to see Father Christmas. Christopher was only a young then and he had cried his little heart out all the way there and back. Mary had struggled to get him to sleep that night and Martin had not been surprised to wake and find him wedged between the two of them.

He swallowed at the memory. And hung his head. Would it ever stop?

"Stanley!" shouted a lady in a paper hat. "You made it! Marvellous, absolutely marvellous. I am glad." She put her arm through Barwell's. He visibly stiffened. "Don't tell Frank I told you so," she whispered conspiratorially, "but the old misery reckoned you wouldn't bother. Thought you'd work all night at that stupid big desk of yours. I told him that was nonsense. I told him that a young man like you wouldn't be staying in on tonight of all nights. And I was right, wasn't I?! I told him you were a good friend and that, knowing how much it meant to him, you would never miss Frank's annual Christmas Eve bash." She was walking Barwell towards the main throng of people. "Not two years in a row," she added.

"Erm, no. Certainly not," said Barwell unconvincingly.

"Well, you're here now, so grab a drink," she handed him a glass of wine from a passing waiter, "and come and meet some people."

"This is truly splendid," said the old man, suddenly appearing beside Martin, an enormous apple in one hand and a piece of Christmas cake in the other. "A magnificent house, don't you think? Have you seen the decorations in the hallway? Superb, simply superb. And you two never wanted to come in. Shame on you," he grinned.

Martin said nothing.

"Christmas, eh?! Everyone's happy celebrating. Makes you wonder why they don't have it more often," jollied the old man.

Martin remained silent.

"Is everything okay?" asked the old man softly.

"Mm, yes," Martin muttered, staring in to his glass.

"You seem a little," the old man placed his hand upon Martin's shoulder, "downcast, my friend."

"No, I'm fine," he replied, and then with a degree of finality added, "As good as ever." He tipped back his head and finished the drink.

Some children ran past kicking a big leather ball. It hit the old man on the leg and bounced across the wooden parquet floor in to the conservatory.

"Sorry, mister," said the eldest boy. He was about six years old with bright ginger hair and trousers torn at the knees. The other children stopped behind him. Martin noticed that some wore conspicuously more expensive clothes than the rest.

"Never mind," replied the old man. He bent down to eye-level with the children. "It's young Terence, isn't it?" The young boy gave him a puzzled look. "Well, you make sure you don't go hitting anyone older than me. We're not all this tough, you know." The children shook their heads in unison. "If you can find anyone older than me that is," the old man chortled. "Now run along and have a wonderful evening. And a Merry Christmas to you all."

"Merry Christmas," they all shouted as one, and then raced off in search of the ball. Within seconds there were the sounds of laughter and tellings-off coming from the conservatory.

"Walk with me, Martin."

"And you remember Alfred, don't you?" asked Frank's wife, Esme.

Barwell nodded hesitantly.

Esme had him firmly by the arm and positioned in the centre of a small circle of people, all of whom he vaguely recognised but none of whom he could name or upon whose life he could shed any light. They were just, well, faces. Some worked for him, he was sure, a few for a fairly long time, and some he recognised from the occasional social event he was required to attend. Certainly none of them were clients.

"How are you Stanley? Haven't seen you since .... must have been that summer bash," said Alfred.

"Yes, I'm well. Thank you." Alfred was a dim memory for Barwell. He could not remember seeing him for a few years at least.

"Business is good, so I hear."

"Yes, fine. And yourself? How's the world of..." Barwell searched the accounts of his mind, "... of iron?"

"Steel?"

"Yes," nodded Barwell.

"Haven't been in steel for ages. I sent you all the details, I'm sure."

"Oh."

"No, I'm in tin now. Nickel and tin to be precise. No one's in steel anymore. You should know, we do enough business together," guffawed Alfred.

Barwell was confused. Perhaps it was the drink. The company had not dealt in tin for eighteen months, ever since he had closed the canning plants.

"Mind you, I do tend to deal with Frank, rather than you. No offence, intended. I've just known him longer, that's all. My type of businessman. Old school. When he retires, and the way he's going he'll be the first man to retire at fifty ..." They all laughed. Esme felt a flush of pride warm her face. "... I'll be more than happy to come through you."

Barwell forced a smile through his thin lips. It must have been the punch and the heady atmosphere. The poor man was living in the past

They were alone now. Martin guessed they were somewhere at the back of the house, although how the old man knew his way through all those twisting corridors and empty hallways, he had no idea. The room was spacious and brightly coloured, and was obviously a playroom of sorts. An assortment of toys and games were spread about the floor together with all manner of sporting bric-a-brac. Scattered amongst these were a multitude of half-eaten cakes, part-flattened chunks of chocolate and shiny bon-bon wrappers, all remnants of a prolonged and boisterous assault on the confectionery table that spanned the entire length of the far wall.

"Have you any children, Martin?" asked the old man.

"Yes. One. Christopher," he replied, as if each word was an effort of concentration.

"How old?"

"Six." He paused. "Or seven."

"Splendid, splendid. It must be wonderful, especially at this time of year."

"Wonderful?" questioned Martin

"Yes, Christmas, Martin. Christmas," bellowed the old man. "Carols by the piano, presents under the tree. The shiver of excitement on Christmas Eve. The ... "

"No, it's not wonderful," interrupted Martin. "It's not wonderful at all."

"It's not?"

"No, it's not." His words were angry, but his anger was not aimed at the old man, it was directionless, at the world in general.

The old man's eyes were large and rheumy and they looked at Martin with genuine concern.

"You do not celebrate Christmas?" he asked gently.

"No," replied Martin, his voice beginning to falter.

"May I ask why?"

"No."

"Fine," accepted the old man.

"Because I hate it," Martin snapped. "It's just a big con. An excuse for getting you to spend money you don't have on things you don't need. Stupid decorations everywhere, annoying songs playing constantly on the radio." Martin finished his drink. He looked at the old man who simply stared at him, unmoved. "Come on, you know what it's like," Martin continued, "All that forced jollity. All happy, happy, happy. Complete strangers wishing you Merry Christmas, as if they know what you're thinking. The family ringing up, inviting you round for dinner, pretending it's all normal, as if nothing's happened. Spoiling Chris with expensive presents." Martin gripped his glass. "I mean, look at this place. All lights and tinsel and people laughing and joking as if it all means something."

"Does it mean nothing to you?" the old man asked quietly.

"Yep. Another year gone, as empty as the last."

Then, without warning, the tears came.

"Whoaar!" shouted Barwell. "This is unfair, surely this is unfair," he moaned stumbling around in the darkness. "Okay, then," he said, as if coming to a decision. "I will make you all pay for this," he roared and then strode purposefully forward, fell over an armchair and landed softly, face first, on to the thick-piled carpet. Everyone watching collapsed in fits of giggles. After several seconds and against all odds, a smile brushed Barwell's face.

"Oh Stanley, you're a wonder. I haven't seen anything so funny in years," said Esme reaching down and removing his blindfold.

It had been a strange night. Esme had seen to it that he had met a tremendous amount of people, all of whom, it must be said, had been inordinately friendly and welcoming. The conversation had, on the whole, been mildly entertaining - light-hearted and lightweight for sure, but not awkward or forced - and he had run in to several people who were important to the company. Strangely enough he had also met quite a few guests who were no longer clients of his but who were equally affable and certainly seemed to bear him no ill will. This was surprising, especially in view of the abruptness of their removal from the company's accounts, very abrupt in some instances. To their credit they appeared to accept the sometimes unkind nature of business with equanimity and managed to talk as if nothing much had changed, although to an uneasy degree in some cases.

"Marvellous, Stanley. Absolutely marvellous," laughed Alfred, patting Barwell on the back.

"Well done, Stanley," said several people he had met earlier in the evening.

The drink had flowed - Esme seemed to treat an empty glass as an insult - and the singing and dancing had become merrier, and the general atmosphere had become one of quite infectious goodwill.

And Barwell, much to his surprise, had found he was rather beginning to enjoy himself. The convivial nature of the conversation no longer tired or intimidated him, although he still kept a dignified distance, and the company gradually grew to be quite agreeable, even Esme; in fact, especially Esme. He would normally have found her manner frighteningly pushy and affected, but he was initially so pleased that she spoke to him at all, given recent events, that he had allowed himself to be led around the party like a lost child, and her generous nature had slowly and irresistibly mellowed his attitude towards her.

Of course, he had still to meet Frank.

"Well done man. Jolly good sport. Ever so funny," said a mountainous man with flushed cheeks and a great grey moustache. Barwell knew him well. He was an important client with whom the company did a huge amount of business.

"Yes, congratulations, Barwell. A great show," smiled his equally voluminous partner, extending his hand. "Must say, didn't think you had it in you. Great spirit. Happy Christmas."

"Oh, yes," stuttered Barwell, red with exertion. "Thank you."

It was Esme, of course, who had called the game of blind man's bluff and had nominated him for the first turn by thrusting the blindfold on his head. If truth were told, his initial reaction was a mixture of annoyance and stupefying embarrassment. It was taking things too far, he felt. He still did. However, his business brain had quickly realised there was no profit to be had in causing a scene and he had decided to play along as well as he could, which given his experience with this sort of thing, was not very well at all. Hence his fumbling failure.

"I'm very proud of you, Stanley. I knew you'd be fine," Esme beamed. She leant forward and kissed him on the cheek. "Are you very angry with me?" she asked demurely.

Barwell looked around at the smiling faces, felt the handshakes and slaps on the back still warm on his skin, thought for a moment and said sternly, "I am."

Esme's eyes dropped and the laughter of the crowd began to peter. Barwell's two clients looked on with disapproval.

"... not," he added with a smile.

Everyone guffawed. The laughter was much louder and more hearty than Barwell's quip deserved, but such was the collective relief that the moment had passed and the high spirits remained.

"Oh young Mr Barwell," said a grinning Esme wagging her finger, "you know, if you go on like this, someone's going to accuse you of having fun."

Awash with boldness, Barwell patted Esme warmly on the shoulder, took yet another glass of punch from the drinks table and sat back and reflected on the first witticism he could remember making for a very long time. As the glow of unaccustomed mirth began to cool, he looked across to his two clients and, remembering his company's motto, tried to calculate how much business for the company his little performance had just generated.

"Nothing earned. Nothing gained," he murmured to himself.

"I am sorry for your loss Martin," comforted the old man. "And I am heartily sorry that this time of year brings the pain back with such force."

"It does not bring it back," said Martin, shaking, "don't you see, it never goes away. All bloody day and night, it's always there, tap-tap-tapping at my brain. This noise it makes, it's deafening." He brought his clenched fist down repeatedly on to the wooden floor, knocking out the rhythm of his grief. "Memories, memories, memories," he thumped.

"Such a bereavement is difficult to bear," said the old man understandingly.

"Yep, tell me about it," Martin sniffed. Then bluntly, "D'you know, I can't go on like this. I know it's normal to be unhappy, but this is different. It's like I've lost the ability to *be* happy." He bowed his head and kneaded the tips of his fingers roughly in to his temples. "I can't concentrate on anything, anything at all. Reading a paper, watching a film, they're all beyond me. I've no interest in going out, I hate staying in. I can't sleep, I dream of not waking up."

The old man nodded sympathetically.

"I never used to be like this, I didn't. I really didn't," he said looking in to the old man's eyes, imploring him to believe him.

"I understand. Things have changed," said the old man gently.

Martin wiped the sleeve of his coat across his face. His eyes were reddened and sore. He nodded to himself.

"You're right," Martin sniffed. "I never used to be alone."

The old man put an arm around Martin's shoulders and felt him shudder with the force of his weeping. The tears came in sets, like waves crashing on a beach, each one formed far away in the maelstrom of his despair and carrying with it the sorrow of his sleepless years. The old man held him tightly as each surge knocked the air from his lungs and left him gasping for breath.

After several minutes the tears began to slow.

"What about Christopher?" asked the old man, suddenly.

"I'm sorry?"

"What about Christopher?"

Martin raised his head from his hands and wiped his eyes.

"Your son?" the old man added.

"What about him?"

"He is part of you, is he not? He is part of you both."

"Yes."

"Then you are not entirely alone," he said as carefully as he could. "You have a child to take care of, a child to love and to look after."

"Please, you've been kind, but I hope you are not presuming to tell me how to care for my son," said Martin. "I know my responsibilities."

"I am not trying to tell you of your responsibilities, Martin, believe me. I am simply trying to help you see that a part of the happiness for which you grieve is still with you. And he needs your love, as much as you do his."

"Chris has my love. He knows that. There is nothing I would not do for him."

"Where is he now, Martin?"

"What do you mean?"

"Where is he now? It is late, it is Christmas Eve, where he? He is not with his father."

"I told you," Martin exploded, "we don't celebrate Christmas. It is not a time of year that we consider special." He spat the word. "For us, it's not a time of happiness." He hesitated for a few moments, trying to calm his breathing. "It's a time of sadness. There's no picture postcard white Christmas for us, I'm afraid. No choirs singing and bells ringing. Just the white noise of silence." Martin stopped and shook his head. And then, quietly, as if to himself, he scowled, "Just a man and his small son, sitting in a hissing vacuum of sound, trying to block out the roar of past celebrations."

He began to cry once more.

Father Christmas waited in the wings of the playroom. He was nervous. He was every year. Silly really. He loved this bit of the party so much, adored so completely seeing all the children's faces when he suddenly appeared in front of them, that he put all his effort in to getting everything just right, and was always disproportionately upset when things went wrong, as they inevitably did each year. And no matter how much everyone reassured him that it was an outstanding success, there was always a part of him that was disappointed, and every year he worked harder in an effort to get it absolutely perfect. So he was nervous.

This year he'd had a new costume made, a beautiful deep green velvet trimmed with white fur. He checked his appearance in the mirror for the umpteenth time. His robes looked good, he had to admit, although the hat could do with a minor adjustment. He tilted it to the left, then a little to the right, and then back to the left. Finally he placed it at the same angle as it had originally been, and gave a little nod of approval.

In a few minutes they should be leading in the children. A couple of minutes for them to settle, and then he would be on. He coughed and practised a few yo-ho-hos under his breath. His throat felt dry. He hoped he was not getting a cold.

"Are you ready Frank?" whispered Esme, poking her head around the thick, purple curtain.

"Are they all in yet?"

"Nearly. There are so many this year. More every year, I'm sure. Must have practically the whole village in tonight. Still, at least it means they enjoy it."

"I know, I can hardly carry the sack, it's so heavy. We'll have to get a sleigh made for next year."

In the half dark, Esme smiled lovingly at her husband.

"How do I look?"

"Darling, you look wonderful. The new costume is splendid. Not that last year's was not splendid too," she added hurriedly.

"Are you sure I have not got too much padding? I'm supposed to be chubby, not rotund. And I think my hat's the wrong size, I can't seem to get it to sit properly. My buttons are ..."

"Frank," interrupted Esme, "you look perfect, absolutely perfect, and I am very proud of you." She leant forward and kissed him warmly on the lips. "Merry Christmas, darling."

"Mind my beard," said Father Christmas nervously, "I don't think the glue is as good as last year."

"Time for the children's show," said Bertram, finishing his drink.

"Yes, come along Stanley, our Ellen is getting a present this year," added Diana, Bertram's wife. "And you two have talking business for a long time now." She raised herself on tip toes to kiss her husband's cheek. "A very long time," she said quietly.

"The children's show?" said Barwell doubtfully.

"Yes, all the children go in to the playroom and meet Father Christmas, and they get a little gift each," replied Diana with a smile, tugging Bertram by the arm and leading him away.

"Sorry, darling. I tried," he whispered. "I don't think he knows anything else."

Diana patted his hand. "Come on, Stanley," she called encouragingly, Bertram's arm clamped to her side. "You'll miss all the fun."

Barwell was undecided. He had drawn a good deal of pleasure from the evening so far, and the last half hour chatting to the Entwhistles had been especially enjoyable. Productive too. But the thought of sitting through a kid's show, full no doubt of small children making a noise and grown men making a fool of themselves, did not appeal. Besides which, it really was time to start heading home.

"Actually, I think I should be getting home now."

"Don't be silly, Stanley," said Bertram, "it is one of the traditions of Christmas Eve. Besides, Esme and Frank would never forgive us if we missed it."

"I'm not sure. It is late."

"Come on, everyone else will be there," said Bertram deliberately.

Barwell thought for a moment. "Okay, lead the way," he replied.

Martin tried to pull himself together. His eyes felt as if they had been dusted with pepper and he wiped them with his handkerchief. His face was hung and pale, and his skin shone with the dull lustre of his tears. He combed his hair forward and bowed his head to hide his dishevelled state from the other party-goers, especially from the children. Through the fringes of his hair he gazed out at a room full of people beaming with joy.

The old man squeezed Martin's knee in a gesture of kinship. They had been deep in conversation when the children had come dancing in, much to the surprise and dismay of them both. There was still more to be said.

"Good evening gentlemen," said Stanley, sitting himself down next to the two of them.

"Good evening, Stanley," replied the old man.

Martin nodded.

"I've not really seen you since we arrived, where have you been?" asked Barwell.

"Oh we've been around," said the old man, "you know, admiring the decorations, drinking the wine, tasting the food." He nodded to a half eaten bowl of hazelnuts on the floor next to him and patted his tummy in a contented way. "Are you enjoying the festivities, Stanley? You certainly seem a might jollier than when I last saw you."

"I must admit it has been a curiously pleasurable evening."

"Ho, ho, ho." The sound came bellowing from the stage. As one, the children fell silent and turned towards the front of the room. "Ho, ho, ho," came the roar again, this time accompanied by the sound of bells. "Merry Christmas! Mer-ry Christmas!" the voice

94

boomed and Father Christmas stepped out in to the light. Thirty pairs of young eyes widened in wonder.

Barwell's eyes narrowed.

"Good God. I do believe that's Frank Torman," he exclaimed.

"Sshh, Stanley," hushed the old man.

"But that's Frank," he said pointing to the velvet clad figure at the front.

"Of course it is."

"But, but ..."

"Stanley lower your voice, you are spoiling it for the children. And please will you sit down."

"But Frank is a well known member of the community," said Barwell, consumed with puzzlement. "He is a respectable business man."

"Was," said the old man sternly.

Barwell ignored the comment. Yet again, deep within him, he could feel the disquiet beginning to stir.

"He does not need to do things like this," he continued. "He seems to be doing fine." Barwell waved to the opulence around him. "Better than I had been led to believe," he muttered. "Surely he could hire someone for this. Someone more appropriate."

"He does not have to do it, you silly, cynical man. He does it because he wants to, I'm told. It's the highlight of his evening. He plans for it months in advance, although, I admit, he seems to have overdone the padding this year. Now sit down and be quiet," growled the old man, reaching up and pulling Barwell down in to the chair next to him.

"So who's been a good boy this year?" enquired Father Christmas, manfully dragging his sack of gifts across the floor.

The quiet was broken by the whoosh of young hands shooting in to the air and an explosion of high-pitched shouting. The adults crammed around the outside of the room smiled broadly.

"And have any of the girls been good?"

More screams, pitched even higher this time.

"He enjoys doing this?" asked Barwell quietly.

Back in the carriage the Sergeant was awake and growing impatient. The fog was clearing and he felt like they should be on their way.

His sleep had refreshed him enormously; it had been long and deep and curiously undisturbed, except by dreams, and he had awoken bursting with life and fired with an urge to push on. Exactly where he felt they should be pushing on to, or, more perplexing, how he had come to be in the carriage in the first place, were questions which occurred to him only fleetingly at the very reaches of his consciousness, where they were buried under the exhaustion of war and his innate acceptance of circumstance forged by nineteen years of regimented living. Occasionally the mists of reason would clear and he would become troubled, but the impulse to continue with his journey pushed any such thoughts swiftly from his mind.

The carriage was warm and his restlessness made it warmer still. He removed the old man's coat from his shoulders. It was a strange garment; thick but not heavy, plainly old but not worn. It was also very warm. In fact, you could feel the warmth radiating off the fur, as if it still covered something with a heartbeat. He wondered where the coat had come from. No great mystery; clothing was being passed around all the time, except for boots. Boots you guarded with your life. It did not look like any uniform he'd ever seen. It certainly wasn't standard issue.

He stood up and pulled down the window and tried to see if there was any sign of imminent movement. Time, he felt, was pressing on him. Mist and darkness met his gaze. There was very little else to see. No platform, no station, no guardhouse.

"Hello," he shouted, somewhat speculatively. His gentle Scottish brogue almost drowned in the watery air. "Hello," he

THE LAST TRAIN HOME

hollered with more vigour. "Is there anybody there?" This time the voice carried, but there was no answer.

He peered in to the gloom for any sign of life, but could see nothing. The stillness was absolute. The only sound was the low hum of silence, like the grains of time falling away. He squinted once more in to nothingness and then closed the window, his new found hunger for life almost unbearable.

Gradually a shadow in the fog coalesced in to the outline of a figure. The Sergeant slammed the window open and shouted at the top of his voice.

"Jingle bells, jingle bells, jingle all the way, ..." sang the children, faces beaming, presents by their side. Father Christmas stood waving his arms on stage, conducting with gusto. His sack lay empty beside him, but he had a smile as broad as his enormous snow-white whiskers, which, as feared, were beginning to peel away from his chin.

"Back to the drawing board for Frank," shouted Alfred, pointing to the loosely fitting beard. "He'll be up all night wondering how to stick it properly for next year."

Esme smiled. All around her people were standing and clapping along to the music.

"Look at him. Forty six years old and still a boy a heart," she hollered above the noise.

"Unlike Stanley, eh?!" nodded Alfred.

"Mm?"

"Half Frank's years but double his age!" he exclaimed.

"Oh, leave Stanley alone," she said defensively. "He's tremendously shy really, and he *has* made the effort to come this year." They both looked over to where Barwell was sitting alone. "He even looks like he's enjoying it." They both laughed.

"Oh what fun, it is to run, on a one horse open sleigh ..."

"Is that your foot tapping, Mr Barwell?" asked the old man in mock seriousness.

Barwell looked down at his feet and then at the old man. His expression was impassive.

"You see that man over there? The big man with the scarlet waistcoat?"

The old man squinted. "Yes."

"He owns the second largest company on the entire East Coast." The old man looked puzzled. "And he's stamping his feet, so I think that the least I can do is tap my toes, don't you?"

For a few moments the old man was speechless, then, at the very edges of Barwell's mouth, he saw a smile appear. He nodded in return.

"Dashing through the snow, on a one horse open sleigh, ..."

Martin wandered through the empty corridors at the back of the house. The sound of singing echoed along the old passageways and was proving inescapable; whichever way he twisted, the singing followed. It was as if it was stalking him, its bubbling levity drawn irresistibly down the emotional pressure gradient to the depression which weighed so heavily upon him.

He'd had to leave. The kids' show had proven too much.

Turning a corner in the dark, the voices finally began to dim. He greeted the silence that rushed in to take their place like an old friend. Release at last. He rubbed his hands across his face and through his hair as if bathing in the solitude. One day, he swore to himself, he would get over this. Gradually his breathing eased, and deepened, and the rapid thudding of his heart began to slow.

He leant against the wall and felt a handle pressing in to his back. Fumbling in the dark, he eventually managed to turn the worn wooden knob and a door opened. He walked through in to the swirling mist and found himself back at the train station.

The singing had finished, the children were playing with their new presents, and Frank had seen them and was coming over. Barwell felt his muscles tense. What would he say? He could hardly be pleased to see him there, despite what he may have told Esme. It had been a harsh thing to tell him that the company would not lend him any money, and deep down Barwell did not feel good about it, but it had been a business decision and a correct one at that. Emotion and charity did not come in to it, and nor should they. However, he did feel awkward enjoying Frank's house and hospitality given how upset with him Frank had recently been. It looked like he was rubbing his nose in Frank's misfortune. Certainly he was not going to believe that they had simply got lost and stumbled on his house by mistake.

He was almost upon them now. Barwell steeled himself for the inevitable tirade.

"Stanley, overjoyed that you could make it," he bellowed, welcoming his old protege with a hug. A small cluster of white whiskers attached themselves to Barwell's cheek where they highlighted the sudden redness of his face. "Are you enjoying yourself?"

"Mm, yes, Frank," Barwell stuttered. "Yes we are very much."

"We?"

"Yes. May I introduce ..." he turned to the old man. There was no-one there.

"Yes?"

"He must have gone to get a drink or something," muttered Barwell, somewhat confused. He was sure the old man was there only seconds ago.

"Stanley. Have you been at the punch? It's wicked stuff, you know. Old Collinton's secret recipe. Won't let anyone in on the secret, just stands there all night ladling it in to poor souls' glasses and watching them go misty-eyed and the like."

"No, I am fine, I assure you."

"Esme tells me you've been entertaining the guests," said Frank with mock suspicion.

"That was Esme's doing," smiled Barwell nervously.

"I rather guessed it might be," laughed Frank placing a velvet-clad, furry-cuffed arm around Barwell and leading him to the dining room. "I am immensely happy that you came, Stanley," he said earnestly.

Barwell felt a small spring of emotion begin to well inside him. It was a strangely unsettling feeling, due largely to its unfamiliarity.

"I am glad that I came," he responded uneasily. He felt it incumbent upon him to broach the subject of their last conversation. "How are you, Frank?" he ventured. "How is everything?"

"I'm fine, Stanley," he replied smacking Barwell on the back. "Thanks for asking."

"Really? Everything has sorted itself out, has it?"

Frank gave Barwell a puzzled look.

"Sorted itself out, Stanley? Not sure I'm with you."

Barwell swallowed. "Last time we met, you were having a few difficulties. Are you sure things are fine?"

Frank smiled. "Stanley, you never cease to amaze me. You're a genius at business, there's no doubt, but you're also a young man. You should have young man's interests, young man's thoughts. Yet your friends and everyone else are here celebrating around you, and all you can think about is some meeting we had at work." A waiter passed with an enormous tray of drinks. Frank took two glasses of punch and gave one to Stanley. "If I'm honest, I'm not even sure which meeting you're talking about. I make it a point never to bring work home with me. Or, I should say, Esme does." Frank tipped back his head and let out a loud and hearty roar. He then turned to Barwell and looked with genuine warmth in to his eyes.

"Stanley, it's Christmas Eve, can things be any other way than fine? Here we are with food fit for the gods and drink fit for," he sniffed at the steaming glass of Collinton's punch he held in his hand, "the adventurous. Music to dance to, friends to laugh with, children to marvel at. It is Christmas, Stanley, the most wonderful time of the year. Things are perfect, my friend. How could they be otherwise?"

"I am welcome, then? I was not sure."

"Stanley, after all that we have been through together, all those late nights working our damnedest just to get the company back on its feet and give ourselves a better life, each one supporting the other, urging the other on ... you are more welcome than anyone. You have truly made my Christmas complete."

Barwell simply did not know what to say.

Still resplendent in his new robes, Frank led his young friend over to the drinks table where they shared a warm glass of punch together and where Father Christmas's whiskers finally let go their precarious hold on his chin and floated to the floor.

"Time to go, Stanley," said the old man, suddenly appearing beside Barwell.

Barwell jumped. "My, where did you spring from?!" he said, startled. He looked at his watch. It showed ten O'clock. "My watch must have stopped," he said, holding it to his ear. "Yes, I suppose you're right, we had better be on our way," he agreed, almost regretfully. "Frank ..." Barwell turned to introduce Frank but found that Esme had dragged him off to a small group of children in the adjoining room. He could see him standing in the middle of the smiling kids, entertaining them with one of his celebrated Yuletide tales. His hands were a whirl of gesticulation as he brought to life the characters of his story. Occasionally, he would let out a thunderous laugh which made his shoulders shake like a jackhammer. He had his back to Barwell, but he could see by the entranced faces of the children that Father Christmas was spinning his magic again once more.

"They look so happy," observed Barwell, without thinking.

"I'm sorry?"

"The children," he reiterated. "Look at them. They seem so happy."

The old man nodded. "It is a good thing. They do not get much opportunity for joy."

"What do you mean?"

"Their situation robs them of many of the simple pleasures of life."

"Their situation?"

"Yes, these are the kids from the lower end of the village. Their young lives are little enriched by money or experience, I'm afraid. They look forward to this all year."

"These are the poor of the town?" asked Barwell in surprise.

The old man smiled and nodded his head. "Frank invites them up here every Christmas Eve."

Barwell was puzzled. He looked over to the children; Frank's broad back quaked merrily as his young audience sat beaming and captivated. He thought of the young boy and girl at the station.

"Where are their parents?"

"Those parents who have not been forced elsewhere to look for work are here."

Barwell looked around the celebrations with increasing astonishment. He could see now that some party goers were decidedly shabbier than others. A brief scan of the room revealed a small but previously unnoticed world of jacketless guests in greying shirts, a jarring horde of frayed cuffs, scuffed shoes and trousers worn thin at the knees. He was utterly mystified by such social mismatching. What on earth would these children's parents have in common with the people here? It was a cruel thing to do.

The old man saw Barwell's face struggling to resolve this human conundrum.

"Stanley, poverty is a state of pocket, not of character. These people are poor, they want for money not for goodness or respectability."

"Please do not lecture me on being poor," he said, struggling to stay composed. "I am well acquainted with penury."

Barwell frowned momentarily as his eye fell upon a rosy faced woman of rustic appearance who thumped past in an outsized dress and shoes of contrasting colours. With a jolt he recognised her as a lady he had been chatting to earlier in the evening.

"Then you of all people should know that their's is a position of ill fortune, not of disgrace," continued the old man.

"Some would argue that their poorness is their disgrace," Barwell ventured. "I was born poor, but with hard work," he clenched his fist as if trying to reaffirm his beliefs, "very, very hard work, I have escaped from that."

"You have done well, Stanley, there is no doubt, and you are to be commended for it. But are we to condemn those who have neither your means nor good fortune? The opportunities you had ..."

"Made," Barwell interjected.

" ... made," accepted the old man, "come more slowly to others, and to some they do not come at all. People are different. Some are not gifted with your drive. Some are, but are shackled by circumstance. Other factors are involved." The old man gestured to the guests talking and laughing in the room around them. "Many of these people have been evicted from their family cottages and have to concentrate all their efforts just on keeping warm. They have no strength left for the pursuit of wealth."

Barwell remembered the tied cottages he had instructed the company to buy. He pictured the evictions: mud, rain, cold, screaming children, swearing mothers, tearful fathers. He recalled assuring everyone that hunger would be their most potent weapon in their subsequent battle with the pickets. The sense of satisfaction he felt on being proven right escaped him now.

"But there is no common ground between them and, and ..." He wanted to say *us*, but he felt the old man's eyes burning in to him. "... everyone else here."

"The common ground is humanity, Stanley, kindness, joy in your fellow man's good health and happiness. These are qualities unrelated to a man's finances. It's what we come together to celebrate. It is what Christmas is all about. Besides, you have been finding common ground quite comfortably with these people for most of the night."

Barwell was confused.

Things did not seem so clear any more.

He looked at the old man and then over at Frank who was still standing in the middle of the circle of children, but who seemed somehow less distinct, almost further away. It must be the drink, he told himself.

"Come Stanley, it really is time to go," said the old man motioning him towards the door.

Suddenly unable to resist the old man's lead, Barwell turned and called to Frank. They were leaving and he felt he could not go without thanking him, and perhaps apologising for recent events. He shouted, but although he heard himself enunciate the words and felt the power of his intent, they seemed to come out as no louder than a whisper. Surely he had not had this much to drink? From nowhere a fine mist, neither cold nor damp, drifted in to the house, rapidly filling the room and drawing a veil over Barwell's vision. He rubbed his eyes vigorously, but to no avail; the mist thickened. He peered around the room. The bright decorations looked suddenly muted, as if drained of colour, and the brilliant white Christmas lights appeared dim and weak. Everything seemed to be fading. He saw Frank turn and squint at them, but there was no recognition. Barwell shivered. He watched as Frank's shape - he was no more than that now - turned very slowly back to the wispy images of the children and then, as the mist closed in, disappear altogether. It was like waking from a dream.

"Goodbye, Frank," he heard himself say.

Within seconds the mist was real and it clung to them like a wet shawl.

"It's getting cold out here," said the old man kindly. "Let's get back on the train. I think it's just about to leave."

14.
HOMELY THOUGHTS

"About flamin' time," said the Sergeant, looking out of the window. "I thought I'd curl up and die if we stayed there any longer."

Martin exhaled, also relieved to be on the move.

The Sergeant turned to the old man. "Young Martin here, reckons I have you to thank for this," he said, holding up the old man's coat.

The old man smiled. "You said you were cold."

"Aye, as well I might have been," agreed the Sergeant. He frowned momentarily as if troubled by something half forgotten, and then piped, "But I'm warm now, fairly burning in fact, and I'll no' be needin' it any more, so you can have it back. Although I am mighty grateful for your kindness and concern," he added. He handed the heavy greatcoat back to the old man. "My friends call me Jock," he said, extending his hand.

The old man shook it warmly. "It is good to see you awake and so full of life, Jock," he said sincerely. The old man made to sit down but the Sergeant remained standing. "Oh, I'm sorry. My friends call me many things," the old man chuckled, "but Mel is the one I prefer."

"Pleased to meet you, Mel, and thank you again."

They all sat down. Barwell stared speechless at the floor.

The Sergeant looked at the old man.

"So Mel, whereabouts in the Empire are you from? You'll not be from these cold parts, I fancy."

The old man glanced across to Martin, who was staring out the window, unhearing.

"I am from many places," he replied.

"We all are, one way or another," said the Sergeant, his clipped tone dismissing such platitudes.

"But you are right," continued the old man, "my heart belongs to warmer climes."

"And where would that be, my friend?" persisted the Sergeant. "Egypt? Persia? Arabia, perhaps?"

"Around those parts," allowed Mel, "though it is a long time since I have been to the land of my birth. Much has changed."

"You're right there. The maps in that part of the world alter at the drop of a hat," said the Sergeant, whose army life in the Middle East had acquainted him with the arcane intertribal politics of the desert sheikdoms and their constantly shifting borders. "Do you miss it, what with being so far away, and all?" he asked in earnest.

"Do I miss it?" repeated the old man in surprise.

"Yes, do you miss it, or are you content with yer memories?"

"It's not something I think about, really," replied the old man with a smile.

"Perhaps you should," advised the Sergeant. "I reckon a part of us never leaves home."

"You may well be right, Jock."

"And it does well to remind ourselves of that every now and then," offered the Sergeant, although he appeared to be unsure why. His forehead furrowed for a few seconds, as if straining to hear a distant voice in a crowd. He then turned and looked out at the window at the nothingness, leaning his head against the cool glass. The low trundle of the train gently shook against his brow. Unthinkingly, he rubbed his hands. "I tell you, Mel. You can be away too long."

For a short time the carriage was quiet except for the lumbering chatter of the train on the rails. The old man nodded along with the rumble of the wheels, glancing briefly at the other three passengers. Occasionally the train would howl through a tunnel and the lights would dim and the carriage would shake, but neither the Sergeant nor Martin nor Barwell appeared to notice. All three sat silent and thoughtful.

"Tell me of your homeland, Mel," said the Sergeant suddenly, still looking out the window.

"My homeland?" asked the old man, slightly taken aback.

The Sergeant turned towards the old man. "Yes, your homeland," he reiterated. "You know, where you grew up. Became a man. Tell me."

"I don't think there's anything to tell."

"Ach, a man like you must have a hundred stories," dismissed the Sergeant. "Warm nights, sticky foods, a thousand smells. I've been there, Mel. Come on, anything to make the journey pass."

"I'm sure there's nothing that would interest you," tried the old man. "A man of your experience."

"Don't worry about me, I'm easily pleased," reassured the Sergeant. "Besides, I've always found a little bit of exoticism takes your mind off things," he added, smiling.

"It's been a long time, Jock. You know how it is. The memory fades."

"You never forget," corrected the Sergeant abruptly. His eyes flickered momentarily and he wiped his palms on his trousers. A smudge of perspiration smeared along his thigh. "And anything's better than sitting waiting here." He leant forward towards the old man and added softly, "If you don't mind, Mel. I reckon I could do with the distraction."

The old man glanced briefly out the window at the cold fog dripping on the glass.

"What would you like to hear?" he asked.

"Anything. Anything that shines in your memory."

"I'll try, but ..."

"Trying's fine."

*

The old man was a reluctant raconteur; it was not a talent for which he was often called upon, he thought. He sat for several minutes toiling at the old, dry land of his past, struggling to rake up some dusty recollections to appease the Sergeant.

It was strange to think of these things, he reflected. Difficult even. Time dims the memory, and it had been such an unimaginable time. But the Sergeant was right; you never forget.

He looked over at Martin and Stanley. Both of them sat without movement, unlistening, lost amongst their own private struggles.

"Ahem," encouraged the Sergeant.

The old man raised his brow and smiled. Then, with a relenting sigh, he sat back, closed his eyes and allowed his mind the luxury of wandering. It was an alien and a slightly disquieting feeling at first and he found it a difficult process; he had, after all, travelled a very long way. But soon the creaking cogs of his memory began to turn more easily, and as the years started to click in to place, they slowly eased open up the huge, time-rusted gates that locked the river of his life. And as a small trickle that breaches a dam rapidly swells in to raging torrent, then so the odd reminiscence grew swiftly in to a surging tide of recollected images and sounds, and soon he was being picked up and washed along on a flood of memories. Back and back across the lifetimes he was taken until he found himself again in a land further away than these people could ever imagine.

"I remember the days were dusty, and the streets were noisy, and the night sky was black and thick with stars," he began. "Strange, it's my childhood memories that stand out the most. It was such a wonderful place to grow up. The days just seemed so … endless. I suppose they always do at that age. I think we must have we played every single minute of every single day, our bodies shiny with sweat and aching with laughter. We used to run through the market dodging between all the traders. Big and ill-tempered, they were. And smelly. Not unpleasant, just earthy, distinctive." Eyes still closed, the old man sniffed the air of the carriage, "A mixture of sweat and desert, and … camel, I think. Anyway we'd scamper along picking up all the fresh figs and dates from under their stalls. Then we'd jump in to the river, walk out until we could just about stand against the current, and eat until our bellies hurt. I can almost feel the sand now squelching between my toes." Instinctively he moved his toes up and down within his boots, squeezing the imaginary riverbed underfoot. "And then there were the palaces, all glittering with gold in the midday sun, so bright that it burned your eyes just to look at them. And, of course, the nomads in their lurid colours, and all the farmers' oxen mewing in the floods, and the whole town dancing at the festival, and …"

He trailed off and opened his eyes.

"O, but listen to me. I'm sure you're not…"

"Carry on, Mel."

"But.."

"Carry on," repeated the Sergeant a little curtly, and then added somewhat cryptically, "I need this."

The old man shrugged, settled back once more and did as he was told. He began again, slowly at first, detailing in hushed and respectful tones the grandeur of the temples. Then, in a more animated fashion, he described the bedlam of the markets. He spoke of being awe-struck by the endlessness of the desert and utterly bewitched by the shimmering beauty of the oases. The games of his childhood, the adventures of his youth and the thrills and trials of life as a young man were all recounted with mischievous glee.

And as the descriptions of his birthplace flowed thickly from his tongue, the more vivid the images became. Places he could scarcely remember, he could now picture vibrant with colour and detail. Long-forgotten characters, nameless and of uncertain

be guiding proceedings. "No idea how you got here, but pleased all the same."

Barwell and Martin stared at each other, dumbfounded. They were still trying to come to terms with the awful scene. The Sergeant sprang forward.

"Sergeant Craig, ma'm. What can we do to help?"

Barwell's brow furrowed in a confusion of emotions. And a flicker of a new one.

"We need people to clear the wreckage, carry the injured, dress wounds and care for the sick. That should be enough to be getting on with, don't you think?" The nurse was a stout woman and wore a stiff, tirelessly starched but threadbare uniform. Upon her chest, camouflaged by the mud and blood of unknown soldiers, the Sergeant could just make out a faded red cross.

"Where are the casualties from?" he asked anxiously.

"The human race," she replied. "Now get on with it, if you please." She pointed to a field table on which lay an array of dressings, bandages and blankets. The Sergeant moved swiftly to his business.

"Sergeant!" shouted the nurse. "Your friends."

The Sergeant looked over at Martin and Barwell who had still not moved.

"Come on you two. The quicker we get things sorted out here, the quicker we can push on."

Martin surveyed the scene in front of him. Something was not right. It had all the hallmarks of a major castatrophe - a rail crash, late at night, thick fog, an inaccessible place - rescue would doubtless be hard and slow. There should be panic, he thought, there should be bedlam. Given the extent and severity of the injuries, there should be moaning and crying. Yet there were none of these. Instead there was an order to it all and the only real noise was the buzz of clipped instructions and busy movement as the medical personnel shuffled efficiently from patient to patient. Also, everyone appeared to be dressed, well, wrongly. And who ever heard of a train acting as hospital transport?

"Martin," shouted the Sergeant. "Jump to it, lad. People are hurtin' over here. They need our help."

This seemed to stir him from his introspection.

"Come on Stanley, we better get going," he said quietly.

"I - I can't" replied Barwell.

"What do you mean, "you can't"?"

"All that blood and dirt and pain," he whispered.

"Stanley, I know it's hard for you. I don't pretend to understand why, but I do know it's hard. I can recognise your pain. But whatever demons you have, you have to put them aside. This is not some kind of inner torment here, this is real. And I know everything seems a little weird at the moment - and, believe me, I'm having problems working it all out - but whatever's happening, people are injured and bleeding, and maybe dying." Martin closed his eyes for a second, concentrating on the task in hand. "We may not be able to do much. Probably can't do anything, knowing me. On the other hand we may be their only hope."

"It's just that ... "

"Now, Stanley. Now. We need to move now." Martin grabbed Barwell by the arm and forced him forward. "We have no choice but to make the effort."

The soldier gripped the old man's hand gratefully, but feebly. He had left most of his strength on the battlefield several days before, spread out in a pool on the frozen ground, and what little remained was oozing from him in a persistent trickle that was gradually turning his dirty-white dressing sodden and red.

"I'll be able to wish God a Merry Christmas personally this year, I think," the young officer whispered between shortened breaths. He was laid out on a stretcher on the damp grass facing up to the sky. He half smiled. "At least they've brought out the stars to greet me."

The old man glanced upwards. Hanging low over the area was a dense canopy of fog, thick and impenetrable apart from a small break in the cloud directly above the soldier. Through the clear black portal of sky glimmered the Milky Way.

"I hope Heaven is as beautiful as they say."

"I'm sure it's as beautiful and peaceful as can be imagined," soothed the old man.

"Good, because I have had my fill of Hell." The soldier closed his eyes. A small tear ran down his cheek, clearing a thin path through the dried mud.

The old man pressed his thick hand firmly against the soldier's forehead. A few moments passed and the soldier's pain appeared to recede.

"It looks like we are going to be here for a while," said the old man, looking around. "Would you like to talk more or get some rest?"

"I think there is precious little left to say."

"Nothing to say? At Christmas?" the old man gently mocked. "There is always something to say at this time of year, my friend."

"Is that so?"

"Most certainly."

"And why should that be?"

"I think it makes up for the silence in between," he smiled.

The soldier remained unconvinced.

"Well, you may as well tell me what you want for Christmas?" the old man persisted. "What is it you secretly wish for?" He leant closer to the soldier's ear. "I promise I will not tell a soul," he added conspiratorially.

The soldier chuckled weakly.

"Unless you are St Nicholas himself, my friend," he said softly, "I think my particular Christmas wish will be left unfulfilled."

"Why? Is it outrageously expensive?" grinned the old man. "Or perhaps outrageously immoral?" he added with a wink.

"Neither, I'm afraid."

"Well, what is it then?" jollied the old man.

The young officer lowered his gaze.

"I should have liked to meet my family once more before I met my Maker."

"I see."

There was a moment of quiet as the soldier searched the lines of the old man's face.

"You see, stranger. Such a small thing to ask, yet so impossible to provide." Even in the soldier's sickly state, he realised he was inexplicably disappointed. "Still, thank you for showing an interest. If you don't mind, I would like to rest now. I am very tired."

The old man looked briefly unto the sky.

"Of course," he said warmly.

He made to stand up from his crouching position and momentarily put out his arm to steady himself. As he did so his hand brushed, unfelt and unnoticed, against the wound on the soldier's leg.

"Sleep well, my friend," he whispered in parting.

Which to everyone's surprise, the soldier duly did. But then it was to be a day of surprises.

The soldier awoke the next morning feeling unexpectedly strong and revitalised, just as the train was pulling in to the station. He pulled himself up from the stretcher with encouraging ease and looked out of the grimy window at the medical personnel and assorted paraphernalia lined up to greet them on the platform, and almost asphyxiated with shock. Standing there amongst a jumble of crates and sacks, stamping their feet to keep warm on this clear and frosty Christmas morn, were his mother, sister and younger brother. He shouted with unbridled joy and then sank in to his pillow, choked with emotion.

Before he could be carried from the train, the nurse arrived to change his bandages. She carefully unpeeled the crusty, crimson dressing from his leg and was astonished to find the bleeding had stopped and the gaping wound was already beginning to heal. Her large, chestnut eyes looked caringly down at the soldier.

"Merry Christmas, Lieutenant," she said. "I think St Nicholas has arrived just in time this year."

The blood trickled down the Sergeant's hand. He shivered.

"You're doing well," said the nurse kindly as she took the dressing from the Sergeant's shaking palm. "This one's finished," she called to the medical helpers, motioning for them to remove the patient, one of many who had needed their wounds redressed.

They had been treating the injured for over an hour now. The Sergeant had been a great help, busily organising a system of treatment and recovery for those less seriously hurt but nonetheless in need of attention. He had quickly taken control of a small area of the crash site and issued polite but firm instructions in such a way that no-one questioned him or, indeed, wondered from where he had suddenly appeared. Instead, they just did as he said, the job got done, and people suffered less. Certainly many young limbs, and some lives, had been saved by his actions. But since the nurse had asked him to help with actually treating the patients, he had grown steadily more quiet and uncomfortable.

"You never get used to it, do you," she said when the young casualty had been taken away. "Been a nurse for fifteen years now. Would have thought I'd seen everything. But no, there's nothing like the sight of unnecessary suffering to put the shock back in to your working life."

The Sergeant said nothing. He was staring silently at the blood on his hand.

"Children they are, most of them. No more than children. They're lucky if it's only their innocence they lose in this war, I can tell you."

Still the Sergeant made no response, but continued wordlessly examining the dripping, scarlet lines on his quivering hand, turning it over and over, as if inspecting for an injury that wasn't there.

"Are you okay?" the sister asked softly. There was no reply. "I asked if you were okay?" she gently repeated, putting her hand on his shoulder.

The Sergeant jumped, startled from his trembling reverie. "What?! O, sorry. Yes, I'm – I'm fine," he stuttered, putting his hand down.

"You seem a little pre-occupied."

For a few moments the Sergeant was silent. Unknowingly he rubbed his hand against his thigh.

"I'm just desperate to get home, that's all," he said eventually.

"Things are beginning to settle here. Shouldn't be long before the rest of the help arrives."

"I need to push on," he added, unlistening. "Need to push on, now. Worried about time. And everything."

"Why the urgency?" the nurse asked.

But the Sergeant had already gone.

"For pity's sake, Stanley, you're going to have to help me with this," cried Martin. He was covered in mud and grease, and was crouching down in the wet earth trying to lift a broken railway sleeper from one of the wheels of the back carriage. The heavy oak block had splintered in the crash and was jutting through the twisted metal of the wheel preventing them from lifting it out of the deep furrow the speeding carriage had cut in the soft ground. It was the last piece of wreckage from this part of the train.

"Can't we just leave it, Martin. We've done our bit, surely," Stanley shouted back.

Stanley was standing far up on the top of the embankment, visibly agitated, with his coat folded over one arm. His jacket was tightly buttoned and his trousers were tucked in to his long woollen socks, each one of which was sopping and filthy. Where his socks ended and his shoes began was difficult to discern. The shiny Oxford brogues were barely visible through the wet brown sludge that clung in clumps to every carefully cobbled indentation in the expensive Italian leather. The smooth, hard-wearing hide from which the soles were exclusively manufactured offered no grip at all on the wet mud and made every slippery step ungainly and unpredictable. This had left him feeling frustrated and useless, imprisoned in his own private ignominy.

"Surely the rescue services will be here soon. There are official bodies to deal with this sort of thing, you know. It's not our job."

"Stanley, come on. You've done well up till now," replied Martin. "One last haul and we can move on."

They had initially been asked to help with the casualties themselves, but Stanley was so obviously distressed by the sight and sounds of the injured that they were swiftly placed on wreckage clearance duties at the far end of the train. Martin did not mind. He was not entirely easy with being so near to such bloody anguish himself, but Stanley appeared to find it genuinely upsetting simply being in close proximity to any human frailties. How on Earth Stanley ran a major successful company whilst lacking any affinity with those less fortunate, which included just about everybody, was a mystery to Martin. It was as if sometime somewhere he had been robbed of the facility to empathise with others.

"No, I've had enough. I'm cold and dirty and I don't want to be here any longer," hollered Stanley. "I've done as much as could be expected of someone in my position and I want to go." The wind was picking up, bitter and northerly, and he momentarily shivered. "I shouldn't be here," he grumbled to himself. "I don't deserve to be here."

"Suit yourself," Martin yelled and turned away, mildly irritated. He lay down on the dripping grass, slid his feet under the sleeper and positioned himself so that he could use his legs to lift the fractured wooden block. He could not work Stanley out. Dirty, physical labour was plainly not something he considered to be within his life's remit, despite the potential human cost at stake here, and having seen him pulling and tugging at the wreckage, it was clear it was not something to which he was naturally suited. Still, he had tried to help, albeit in a somewhat ineffectual way, and Martin got the impression that he would have toiled longer and harder if only he was not so useless at it. Inadequacy probably did not sit easily on the shoulders of such a young and successful captain of industry, he reflected. On the other hand uselessness and Martin had become intimately acquainted over the past few years and to be able to rid himself of such a feeling, even if it was only for a short time and in such terrible circumstances, was proving an unexpected relief. If truth be told, he was a little enjoying himself, he thought guiltily.

Martin shuffled his feet to get greater purchase on the block, tensed his legs and heaved the large wooden slab in to the air. The wheel fell away with a clatter, but two of its twisted iron spokes caught on the large oaken splinter that jutted from the side of the sleeper and the wheel just hung there. The weight of both the sleeper and the wheel pressed down on Martin's legs with the force of a truck. It was too much to hold. He cursed. Then he heard the call.

"Help! Please help!" said a frightened voice. It was muffled and breathless, and nearly lost amongst the soft muddy walls of the ditch in which the wreckage sat. "Help me, please!"

"Is somebody there?" Martin shouted, his legs beginning to tremble with the weight.

"Yes, yes. O God, thank you, thank you. Please. Help me get out of here."

"Stanley!" bellowed Martin. "Quick, I need you here now."

Stanley did not answer. He simply folded his arms demonstratively and sat down on a large rock, shiny with rain.

"Can you pull yourself up?" Martin called to the unseen casualty.

"My leg's broken, but I think I can drag myself out." He sounded young, still in his teens. "There's a space now. I'll try."

Deep in the ditch amongst the tangle of mud and metalwork, the injured man began his painful climb. The initial adrenalin surge had now passed and Martin partially relaxed for the briefest moment, and then suddenly became aware of the huge weight pushing down on his legs and back. He was not in the best position to hold the block; his back was twisted awkwardly and his legs were fiery with the strain.

"No, wait a second. It's too heavy. I need to adjust my footing," he shouted in alarm.

"Sorry, did you say something? I didn't get ..."

Martin's knees buckled.

"Aargh," screamed the youngster as the jagged metal once more pinned his leg to the ground. Above the noise of the young man's wailing, above the noise of the wind, Martin heard the bone shatter.

"I'm sorry," he cried. "I'm sorry. I couldn't... Are you okay?"

"O, Lord," gasped the voice. "I – I can't breath. I can't breath. Help me."

"Stanley," Martin yelled again. "Stanley, get down here." Then, to the injured man, "Don't worry, I'm going to get you out of there," he reassured, trying desperately to sound in control. Martin was panting heavily now. Sweat trickled from his forehead and stung his eyes. He tried to wipe it away with his sleeve, but succeeded only in smearing mud across his face. "Okay, stay calm," he told the young man, "I'm going to try to lift it again."

Still lying on his back, Martin wedged himself as far forward as possible so his knees were bent right under the wooden sleeper. He closed his eyes and tensed. And as always during these moments, when the night was filled with troubles, the doubts flooded in. Would he be able to lift it again? He swore he felt something tear in his knee when it collapsed. Please, not the cartilage again. What would happen if he couldn't lift it up?

"Please. My chest. I'm pinned down," came the desperate and breathless call.

Martin roared and thrust his legs upwards with every trace of strength left in his tired body, and the sleeper lifted. He quickly locked his knees, although they juddered violently with the effort.

The voice howled.

"Please, you'll have to hurry. I can't hold it for long."

"I – I don't know if I can move."

"I'm sorry. You'll have to. And you must be quick."

Martin lay back and concentrated on trying to block out the burning in his legs. The agonising sounds of the injured man beginning to drag his broken frame through the serrated maze of wood and metal were a powerful distraction. The small opening that Martin's efforts had made in the wreckage swelled and shrank like a heaving chest as his legs shook with pain. He craned his neck backwards.

"Stanley, there's someone trapped down here. I need you now. I can't hold it by myself." Stanley hesitated.

"Please, Stanley," Martin bellowed, "someone's down here. Honestly. My legs. I can't hold it for much longer."

Up on the embankment, a wary and reluctant Stanley appeared to make a decision. He lay his coat down on the rock on which he sat and began to edge his way down the treacherously slippery slope. Clearly unconvinced by Martin's assertions, he was in no hurry to embarrass himself.

"I can see the gap. It's not easy," the voice panted.

"Just keep moving as quickly as possible," rasped Martin, his teeth clenched. "Whatever you do, don't stop." He looked back to the embankment and growled, "Come on, Stanley. Come on."

Stanley was nearer now and he could see Martin's face swollen with exertion as he struggled to keep the huge sleeper aloft. Clearly, this was real. Panicked seized him. He immediately tried to hurry, but stumbled and slid bottom-first along the sodden ground to the foot of the embankment. He punched the wet earth, boiling with uselessness and humiliation.

"Are you there yet?" called Martin to the young man.

"Nearly," he wheezed. "Just a moment more."

Martin's legs were aflame. His brain was screaming at him to let the weight go.

"I- I can't hold on much longer."

"Please, I am nearly through," the voice pleaded.

The youth's hands emerged from the wreckage and frantically grappled back and forth, desperately feeling around for a safe handhold to pull himself out. Everywhere there were razor edges and jagged spikes.

"Just pull yourself up. We'll deal with everything else later. Just get out of there."

"I'm trying, I'm trying. Please hold on."

"Quick, quick, my legs are going." Martin's legs were now shaking uncontrollably as they begged the remaining oxygen from his muscles. Within seconds they would exhaust their energy supply and no amount of willpower would keep them pushing. "Stanley!" he screeched.

Stanley was now running, but the saturated earth meant that he spent as much time clambering to his feet as he did moving forward. His suit was ruined.

"Nearly there," the voice shouted.

Through his half-closed eyes, bulbous and veiny with effort, Martin could see the young man's upper body. He was going to make it. They were going to make it.

"A few seconds more. Nearly out."

Martin could no longer feel the pain. His legs were numb and his brain was drifting. He would need a bath tonight, he thought in his delirium.

Suddenly a scream echoed through twisted carcass of the carriage.

"No. No," cried the terrified youth.

"What's wrong?" shouted the Sergeant, suddenly appearing out of the dark, sliding along the sopping earth.

"O Jesus. My leg is stuck. I can't move."

Martin's knees gave way and he passed out.

"You'll be fine now, lad," said the Sergeant. The young man was lying on a stretcher, his crushed leg roughly splinted against a shard of wood from the railway sleeper. The medical helpers had done a good job, guided at every step by precise instructions barked by the Sergeant.

"How about you? Is your back okay?" asked the youth.

"Aye, fine. Can't feel a thing."

And the strange thing was, the Sergeant was being truthful. He couldn't feel any pain in his back. Or his legs, for that matter. Which was peculiar, to say the least. In view of the fact that he had held the combined mass of the sleeper, the wheel and other assorted weighty debris on his back for nearly two minutes whilst the young man had freed his leg and hauled himself painfully to the surface, it was nigh on a miracle.

"Thank you. Thank you, so much, Jock." The young man was drifting in and out of consciousness now. "And thank your friend, please," he added, his eyes motioning to Martin who sat hunched over in some discomfort several yards away. Stanley was trying to help him, but was clearly unsure what to do. Martin sat kneading his legs and grimacing, while Stanley, his bespoke clothes buttoned tightly, fussed around ankle deep in the soaking mire, a man truly out of his depth.

The Sergeant sighed.

"Of course, I will," he soothed, but the youth had already lapsed in to unconsciousness.

The Sergeant rubbed his back. He knew his spine should be throbbing, broken even, but it was not, it was simply numb. No pain, no feeling at all. Perhaps it was the adrenalin, he thought to himself. He'd seen many men returning from battle with gaping, painless wounds and, in one case, a hand unknowingly shot off. Of course, they had paid for it later, paid for it dearly when the overwhelming stimulus of self survival had receded. May be that was it. Perhaps his back was anaesthetised by the overpowering need to get home. In which case, there would be an awful price to pay later.

All of a sudden the youth gripped the Sergeant's hand.

"And Merry Christmas to you both," he said drowsily. "I hope you make it back."

Before the Sergeant could ask what the young man meant, he had passed out once more and was being stretchered away by the helpers.

16.
ICE

"Are you okay to move?" asked the Sergeant.

"Yes, I think so," replied Martin uncertainly. "Knees are still a bit …"

"Good, let's go," he insisted.

The wind was blowing strongly now, whistling through the railway cutting. It was icy and smelt of snow.

Stanley removed a sopping handkerchief from his jacket pocket. "Excuse me, can I just have a moment to dry myself down?" he enquired haughtily.

"No time," clipped the Sergeant, and strode off up the embankment.

Martin shrugged, gingerly tested out his legs and followed hesitantly.

"Come on, Stanley," he called back. "We all want to get home, don't we?"

Stanley wiped his handkerchief across his face and hands, and then, in a futile attempt to clean himself, tried to brush some of the mud from his jacket; the sodden cotton simply smeared the sludge over a greater area. He cursed.

"This really is the longest night I've ever known," he grumbled and then trudged off after the others.

They were walking along the top of the embankment now. It was very cold up here, much more so than down in the frantic bustle of the crash site. A thick hoar frost already coated the ground and the soft earth was frozen in to jagged ruts that made walking slow and hazardous. Martin's knees were still sore and complained bitterly as his ankles twisted in and out of the icy furrows. Stanley straggled far behind, steam rising steadily from his undershirt, moaning silently and ceaselessly to himself. He was sweating profusely, and when he stopped to catch his breath, the wind whipped the damp from his clothes and the warmth from his body, and he begun to shake violently with the cold. In front, the Sergeant marched purposefully forward, crunching the soil underfoot, at home in the terrain of the trenches.

"Jock, can we please just wait a minute," called Martin.

The Sergeant stopped and looked back.

"Please," implored Martin.

"Ok, then. Just a minute, mind," he conceded reluctantly.

Stanley eventually caught up with the two men, stumbling and swearing along the rough track, his mood sinking with every step. He had retrieved his coat from the rock, but it provided little warmth. The gabardine material was saturated and both sleeves had picked up small tears around the elbows where Stanley had snagged them on the thorny branches that overhung the path. He had also grazed his hand tripping on the spiky, iron earth, and he unrolled his grubby handkerchief and dabbed at the tiny scuffs in his palm; he winced as much in frustration as in pain.

The wind was now gusting, lashing along the crest of ground in biting, polar blasts. The borders of the embankment were thickly wooded and the three men stepped in to the trees for shelter, but winter's grip was harsh and unremitting up on this exposed plateau, and the trees' skeletonised branches, denuded of all vegetation, offered little resistance to the glacial squalls. They walked deeper in to the wood, but the wind eased little.

"That was a good thing you did back there, Martin," said the Sergeant.

"Thanks," he replied, stamping his feet and trying to blow some warmth in to his hands. "Lucky you turned up when you did."

"Where were you, Stanley?"

The abruptness of the question caught Stanley momentarily off guard.

"Where was I?" he spluttered.

The Sergeant nodded.

"I - I was traipsing through a filthy quagmire trying to get there, if you didn't notice."

"I mean, why were you not there already?"

"It wasn't exactly easy to move in that mud, especially in these clothes. It took time."

"No, why were you not there already," the Sergeant repeated, "helping Martin to clear the debris?"

"I don't see what business it is….."

"This is not business, Stanley. Why were you not down there helping Martin?"

"Why was I not down there?" Stanley half-repeated, an air of desperation in his voice. The Sergeant said nothing. Stanley made to answer, but his response trailed off almost immediately. He then stared at the ground for a few moments. When he looked up again his expression was stern, his back straighter.

"Because I'd had enough," declared the head of Torwell Industries. "I'd already done as much as I could, and I was freezing and filthy, and I'd had enough. I work hard all day and I was tired and I simply did not want to help any more, did not see why I should. Is that okay for you?" he demanded irritably.

The Sergeant raised an eyebrow, but remained silent.

"I'm now going to find our train, wait for the line to be cleared and hopefully I'll wake up at home and none of this indisputably strange night will have happened."

"Who brought you up, son?"

The question scythed through Stanley's bluster.

"What on Earth has that got to do with anything?"

"I just wondered," said the Sergeant, "because no son of mine would ever behave like that. Five seconds later and that lad would've been crushed. And all because you'd 'had enough'. Did your father not teach you anything?"

"Unlikely, he died before I was born," Stanley sniped. The anger was beginning to rise; anything to suppress the guilt. "And to answer your question, no-one brought me up. I did most of it myself."

"That explains a lot."

Stanley erupted. "Does it?! Does it now? Please tell me how, Sergeant, because I'm fascinated. You clearly know so much about my life having met me only an hour ago."

"You brought yourself up. Says something."

"Says something?!" repeated Stanley, and then more loudly "Says something? About what? You don't know the first thing about me."

"Reckon I've idea enough."

"You have no idea at all," Stanley growled.

"I know what you did, your background," clipped the Sergeant. "I'm just saying, it explains a lot"

"You think you know me because you think you know my background? You think that explains *me*, does it?" Stanley's voice was raised, but most of the fury was carried away on the rushing wind. "Well, of all the presumptuous ..... Don't you assume you know anything of my background," he raged.

The Sergeant stared at Stanley, unmoved.

"So what does it explain then? Come on, Sergeant, let's hear it. What lies have you heard, what assumptions have you made? I've heard them all. Let me guess - born rich, eh? Well, unless you count twenty different homes in the first eight years of my life as making us rich, then you're wrong. Think, again." Stanley prodded his finger in to his temple to emphasize the point. "Ok, how about - an easy life with a cosy upbringing?" Stanley spat. "Sorry, lies again. Just one grey town after another, I'm afraid. Bellies never full, pockets always empty. What else? Come on, Sergeant, there must be more, there's always more. How about, let's see, I never did anything myself, someone else provided the talent, the drive? Now that would have been impressive, seeing as we were never anywhere long enough to say anything beyond hello and goodbye, let alone make any friends. The creepy landlords that followed us around were not generally given to helping a young boy get on in life, and the parade of suitors outside my mother's door....." Stanley momentary slowed, but then, catching himself, he scowled, "As for family, well, the back of my aunt's hand across my face helped me understand something, but it was nothing to do with business, I can assure you. So, tell me Sergeant, a man of such obvious experience and wisdom, does it explain all of that? Does it? Please, tell me, because I am dying to know."

"No, it just explains why you always think of yourself."

Stanley was momentarily stupefied in to silence.

"Oh," he murmured.

He stood staring blankly at the Sergeant, the wind buffeting his cheeks as he sought for an answer. Then the rain hit him. Not normal rain, but a freezing deluge, blown in from the north, superchilled by the tundra and pack ice of the Artic. The thick droplets froze immediately on impact with the frosty ground and within minutes there was a thin layer of solid ice covering everything on which the storm fell. The branches of the trees were already beginning to bend.

"Ice storm," said the Sergeant. "Real problem. Need to push on as much as we can before the ice gets too thick." Without warning, the Sergeant began to stride off.

"The train's this way," Martin called.

The Sergeant turned. "That's not goin' anywhere until they clear the track, which won't be for a day or two at least."

"We'll just wait until the rescue services come, then."

"Aye, we can wait hours in a freezin' train with no power, or we can walk to the next station and grab a lift from there."

"Do you know how far it is?"

"Can't be that far. Seemed like miles from the last station."

Martin hesitated. The ice was building underfoot. He began to walk towards the Sergeant, but then stopped.

"Jock, don't you think we should, you know, have a talk," he shouted above the wind.

"About what?"

"About all of this."

"All of what?"

"This," Martin hollered in to the gale, waving his arms. "I mean, come on, something's not quite right, is it? Hospital trains and houses with secret passageways to stations? That's not normal, in my book. And there's everything else too. Look at you, clearly a well-travelled and intelligent man, but you seem to have no idea where you're going and if you did, it wouldn't matter anyway, because the train doesn't seem to stop anywhere known to British Rail. The only person who seems to know anything is Mel, and he's suddenly, and conveniently, disappeared. On top of which, Stanley's got a haircut like my grandad." The freezing rain bashed against the two men. "Snappy dresser, though."

"I do know where I'm going, Martin," replied the Sergeant in a solemn tone. "It may slip my mind sometimes, but, believe me, I do know."

Martin shrugged. "Ok, what about everything else?"

"What do you mean - everything else?"

"The whole night. You know, unusual trains and chance meetings and peculiar crashes, not to mention a whole cast of extras from O What a Lovely War. Don't you think it's a bit," he searched for the right word, "well, strange."

"No, I don't."

"What, not at all?"

"No."

"I mean, even the weather's weird. It hasn't stayed the same for longer than a few minutes."

"You suspect the weather now?"

"No," replied a struggling Martin. "O come on, Jock, you know what I'm talking about. At the very least, you have to admit it's been a little odd."

"Granted, the night might seem a little disjointed, but emergencies and panic under a brooding sky do that to a man. Also, we all seem to be desperate to get home and desperation can do funny things to person's mind. I've seen it. It confuses things, mixes them up. It's like a drug."

"Or alcohol," Martin considered.

"Aye, a bit of scotch on a dark night and the world can tip on its axis."

"Perhaps."

"Martin, believe me, lad, I've seen much worse and a lot stranger nights that this one. And I was no' prepared to die of exposure then, and I don't see why I should now. So why don't we head for the next station, get a lift home, and the feelin' back in our toes, and I bet you the sun will come up in the morning." He then added, "whatever haircut Stanley has."

Martin glanced down at the ice forming on his clothes.

"Right, Jock, you win," he said relenting, but unconvinced. "I admit Christmas Eve is not the best time to be sitting around waiting for someone else to help you out. It makes sense to move on. But..." He waved his finger half-jokingly at the Sergeant. "I tell you, they better have a phone at the station."

"A telephone? A working telephone at a station? Perhaps you are dreaming, after all," the Sergeant said, half-smiling.

"Yep, you're right. We should be so lucky, eh?!"

Martin stuck his hands in his pockets and tucked his chin in to his coat.

"Ok, the odyssey continues. Let's walk."

"How about you, Stanley?" asked the Sergeant.

Stanley stood a few yards away looking at the ground. The freezing rain bounced off his upturned collar as he stared vacantly downwards, oblivious to the other men. His argument with the Sergeant had left him stranded in a painfully silent world of conflicting emotions, a world that was utterly alien to him and with which he was ill equipped to cope. At short time ago, he would have harangued the Sergeant for being so knowing about his background, but now, well, he did not know what he felt any more. He was angry and affronted, guilty and battered. He was also sulking.

"Stanley," the Sergeant repeated. "Are you coming with us? It'd be a bit dangerous to go back by yourself in this weather."

"Shouldn't we wait for the old man?" he meekly replied. He was worn down and it was all he could manage.

"I wouldn't worry too much about him. Something tells me he's bound to turn up at some stage," said Martin, now fully immersed in the unfolding adventure of the evening.

Without a word, Stanley simply hugged his coat more tightly around him and set off walking through the wood, shuffling and stumbling as he went, as bedraggled and forlorn a figure as could be imagined. The Sergeant and Martin looked at each other in surprise and then quickly followed.

The passage through the wood back to the embankment was a difficult one. The rain was heavy and constant; it was not uncomfortable, its magical transformation to ice snared the usual splash and spray, but it did make it hard to see. Navigation was made even more tricky by the lattice work of frozen puddles which covered the ground, as the storm quickly filled the troughs and depressions of the churned-up soil. The three men tried to stay on a straight path but were soon forced in to skirting round the side of these mini rinks or hopping from one pinnacle of frozen earth to the other. The lack of reference points was also proving to be a problem. Every shrub and every tree looked the same, petrified in a dazzling coat of white.

Ten minutes later they had still not found the track and tempers were becoming frayed as the cold began to gnaw. And then, as swiftly as it had started, the rain stopped. The wind eased and for a while all that could be heard was the breathless panting of the three men. After a few moments, the clouds scurried apart, revealing a watery moon. The pale moonshine glazed the wood with light and glistened off the sparkling crystal garden the storm had created, and each man stopped to marvel at the stark and dangerous beauty of this winter wonderland in which they were now clearly lost.

"Beautiful, isn't it?" said the old man, suddenly appearing.

"Right on cue," chimed Martin.

The old man stood beaming at them from a small clearing in the wood. He had apparently waded through the trees as blindly as them, because hundreds of tiny ice crystals had caught on his clothes and beard, and they cut and twisted the pallid light of the moon to such an extent that he practically twinkled.

"It's like a wonderland, don't you think?" suggested the old man.

"Yep, curiouser and curiouser," Martin whispered to himself.

"I'm glad I found you," said the old man.

"Where have you been?" asked Stanley

"Helping the injured. How about you?"

And there it was again, thought Stanley, looking sheepishly at his feet; a simple question, apparently asked in all innocence, yet immediately disconcerting.

"So have we," Martin kindly interjected. "We're trying to get to the next station."

"I need to get home," said the Sergeant.

"I think we all do," Martin added.

"Can you help, Mel?" asked the Sergeant.

"I don't think you need my help, Jock," replied the old man softly. "But I would like to join you. If you don't mind, that is."

Martin smiled. "It wouldn't be the same without you."

Suddenly Stanley pointed to a light in the East. "There's something over there. A light, I think," he boomed.

"Yes, that's got to be it," rallied the Sergeant. "Let's go then. Need to hurry, it's gettin' late. Let's just hope the storm holds off."

Martin nodded at the old man.

"Told you."

17.
COLD

But the Sergeant's hopes were in vain, the storm did not hold off. It blew and poured more powerfully than before, as if the brief lull had helped it gather its strength.

They had left the wood several minutes earlier and had set out across a frozen field made flat by the ice and coloured a lustrous silvery-white by the dull moonlight. They were only a little way across when, like a patient sniper having lured its target in to the open, the bitter wind arced around the wooded edge and began to unleash its icy cargo on the exposed men. Soon the moon was gone, the wood had disappeared and the only way to go was blindly forward.

"This night," Stanley panted, shaking his head, "this night is the most exhausting night of my life." He slid unsteadily forward on the ice. "In every possible way."

"We'll be there soon," said Martin kindly.

"You'll forgive me, if I believe that when I see it. I'm beginning to think I am cursed to live in this infernal night forever. Never washing, never drying. Always moving, always tired."

Martin smiled. Stanley looked up from his precarious path.

"I get the impression, Martin, you find me amusing somehow."

"Amusing?" replied Martin, with a wry grin.

Stanley nodded. "I suspect so."

"Well, may be, but not in an unkind way," assured Martin, nearly tripping on an icy divot. "It's just, you know, you make me laugh."

"I must say, I'm not used to providing such entertainment for others."

"That's the sort of thing I mean – 'I'm not used to providing such entertainment for others'" Martin mimicked, laughing.

"I'm not," Stanley puffed.

"No, it's the things you say. I mean, you're only young, you're younger than me. Yet you speak and act like some ageing gentleman. How did you get so old?"

Stanley turned abruptly around, a severe look on his face, but almost immediately his expression softened. "If I appear older to you, Martin, it is probably because circumstances have dictated so."

"I can understand that," said Martin sympathetically.

"Business requires a mature mind."

"Oh, I'm sure it does, Stanley. I'm sure it does. But I still maintain you haven't been around long enough to let life wear you down in to such a grumpy so and so," Martin joked. Seeing Stanley's harsh expression, he quickly added. "No offence meant."

Stanley sighed. "I just am, who I am, Martin," he replied, brushing ice crystals from his trousers. "I'm sorry if my demeanour does not lend itself quite so readily to humour as yours."

"I still reckon there's happy soul hiding in there some where."

"May be, but I wager it will struggle to reveal itself tonight."

Martin squinted ahead in to the freezing rain. "Now that, I can understand."

The men forged on against the hissing wind.

"Do you think it's much further?"

"Not sure," Martin replied. "How much further do you think, Jock?" he shouted.

"It can't be far," enthused the Sergeant, marching and skidding ahead of the rest. "A mile at the most. We just need to keep moving."

"It's freezing. It's hard to see," Stanley called. "Perhaps we should turn round. Go back to the woods for shelter?"

The Sergeant turned on him. "No," he snapped.

"But, we don't know…"

"No. We keep moving," the Sergeant ordered. Stanley stared at him, desperately trying not to look cowed, but the cold and dirt and fatigue had severely weakened his resolve. The Sergeant relented. "Look I'm sorry if … I don't mean to be so abrupt, son. It's just that, I have to get home. There's not much time left."

"So you keep saying," said Stanley. "But I don't understand. There's not much time left before, what, the last train home? When your leave ends? Before I finally get a bath? What do you mean? There's not much time left before *what?*"

The Sergeant looked at him.

"Does it matter?"

"Yes, it bloody well does."

The Sergeant rubbed his hands through his hair and clamped shut his eyes, his heavily-lined face seemingly straining with effort. Stanley looked over to Martin, who simply shrugged.

Then painfully and quietly, barely audible in the wind, the Sergeant growled, "I don't know." He then turned on his heels and began marching off again. As he stomped away, he whispered to no-one in particular, "Before there's no time left at all."

Never had Stanley seen a man so driven and distressed by something so unknown. It was very unsettling.

Stanley watched the Sergeant go, the raw wind blustering against his face. The storm was closing in on them and it was hard to see anything beyond the three men now. The rain was pelting and freezing, and the droning wind moaned around them, hemming them in. It made the night appear darker somehow. Perhaps it was the weather, Stanley thought, or the exhaustion, or just this interminable night, but whatever was pressing down on the Sergeant was beginning to press down on them all. They all needed to get the station, to get to the light.

"I can't see it any more," Martin hollered above the wind. "The light, I can't see it any more."

"Don't worry," the Sergeant called back. "The storm's just getting heavier. It's bound to affect visibility. Let's push on."

"How do we know we're walking in the right direction?"

"Trust me. I've done this before."

"But we could be walking in circles."

"We're not. We simply keep on the same heading. Follow me and keep moving,"

"But…"

The old man patted Martin warmly on the shoulder. His voice effortlessly cut through the noise.

"Martin, we *are* going the right way," he reassured.

"Are you sure?"

"Absolutely."

Martin relaxed.

Suddenly a loud crack, like the snap of a rifle shot, punched its way through the whining wind. Instinctively the Sergeant dropped to the ground. Martin automatically followed suit, but then immediately felt ludicrous and jumped to his feet pretending he had simply stumbled. The old man looked on bemused.

"What was that?" asked Martin.

"Sounded like a gunshot," replied the Sergeant.

"Are you kidding? Why would anyone be…."

"Is everyone okay?" the Sergeant shouted, getting carefully to his feet. No reply. "I said, is everyone okay?" he called again, more urgently.

"Eh? Yes, Jock, yes, I'm fine," said Martin, completely bewildered.

"Me too," acknowledged the old man.

"How about you, Stanley?"

There was no answer. Stanley had disappeared.

*

Numbing cold. Deadening, absolute, numbing cold. Cold to stop the breath and arrest the heart. Stanley was cold. And, he thought, wet. What little sensation that remained in his body, what few sparks of tactile awareness that had not yet been icily anaesthetised, seemed to be detecting that he was wet. Wet and moving. And most definitely drowning.

He was not gasping for air. His body was not thrashing wildly as it begged desperately for a few last snatches of oxygen. This pleased him. Soothed by the cold, his brain had been lulled in to demanding only sleep. Not his normal sleep; a beautiful sleep, undisturbed by dreams or by dark disappointments.

His eyes were dimly aware of a muted, bluish hue as his body swept rapidly along under the ice. Occasionally they vaguely registered a darker shape through the mottled dullness, as if something, or someone, was moving along with him.

How peaceful it was, and how quiet, silent except for the comforting whoosh of the water as it rocked him to sleep and hushed him to be still, and the brief but rapid thuds on the ice above. It was quite pleasant really. In some ways it was a relief, especially after all these years. Finally, a happy Christmas, his barely conscious brain considered.

Then a light, painful and piercing, stabbed through the darkness, a frayed rope rubbed at his unfeeling skin and a young hand pulled him rudely from the silence up in to the howling night with uncommon strength.

The last thing he remembered was a donkey.

18.
THOMAS AND GRANDMA

"Quick, grandma, quick," the young lad called frantically. "The fire. Build it up. Build it up."

"What's wrong? Did you get the wood?" said grandma, shuffling in to the living room from the tiny kitchen.

"Yes, grandma," he replied, throwing a sack of rough-cut logs on to the cold stone floor. "But a man fell through the ice." Behind him, the Sergeant was carrying Stanley through the door of the small cottage. He was wrapped in the old man's coat and mumbling incoherently through the fur-lined hood. The skin of his face was clammy and his lips were blue. "I pulled him out, grandma. Me and Rosa, we pulled him out. He is very cold." The young lad was beginning to wheeze.

"Slow down, Thomas, slow down," she said, calming the boy. "Remember what we said." She put a thin, bony hand on Thomas's shoulders and after a few hissing puffs, he began to relax. "Remember, deep slow breaths. There's no reason to get all flustered."

The old woman motioned to the Sergeant to place Stanley on the large, tattered armchair next to the fire.

"But grandma, we pulled him out. I had to catch him. Rosa needs feeding."

"I know. You can tell me about it in a minute. Now calm down, and then go and get the big iron pot. You know, the one at the back of the scullery. Fill it with water and bring it in here."

"But Rosa will be hungry."

"Rosa is always hungry. She can wait a little while. Now a few more deep breaths and go and get the pot." The young lad made a show of two shallow pants and sprinted off to the scullery, buzzing with enthusiasm. Immediately the sounds of metal clanging filled the room. The old woman looked at the Sergeant. "He tends to get a bit over excited."

"Aye, I can see."

"It's not good for him. Now let's have a look at your friend."

The old woman was dressed in a threadbare woollen dress tied at the waist with a piece of hessian; the same material was wrapped bucket-like around her feet. Over her shoulders she wore a thick, black shawl which she carefully unpinned and lay over the old wooden stool next to fire. She bent down and placed a delicate, veiny hand against Stanley's forehead.

"How long was he in the water?" she asked.

"Not much over a minute. Two minutes at the most. We didn't know where he'd gone at first. Just heard a crack."

The old woman nodded understandingly. "The ice is thin on the lake this time of year. It can snap like that." She clicked her bony fingers. "He'd disappear in an instant. You would struggle to see anything in this storm. What's your friend's name?"

"Stanley."

She took both Stanley's hands and placed the palms against her cheeks.

"And yours?"

"Jock."

"He's very cold, Jock. Another thirty seconds and he'd have been gone."

The Sergeant swallowed. "But he'll be okay?" he asked nervously.

"Should be fine." The Sergeant's relief was deep and heartfelt. "Take off his clothes."

"Sorry?"

"Take off his clothes. They're soaking wet and sapping what little warmth that's left straight out of him."

"Are you sure? It just seems a little….."

"Take off his clothes now or he'll die."

The Sergeant knew an order when he heard one and immediately started stripping Stanley of his sopping garments.

"Got it, grandma," shouted Thomas, limping in with the heavy pot. Behind him there was a trail of small splashes marking his manful struggle from the scullery. "I've filled it with water, like you said. Spilt a bit. Sorry."

"Good boy, Thomas. Put it down there. Now go and get the big towel hanging over the stove."

"The big brown one?"

"Yes, that's it. Be quick about it."

Within seconds the young lad had returned with the thin cotton towel. It was old and very worn in places, but was clean and warm. The old woman handed it to the Sergeant who had swiftly stripped Stanley down to his long johns.

"Dry him down with this. Dry him very well," she said. The Sergeant began to rub Stanley vigorously with the brown towel. "Then take off your coat and get on the chair next to him and hug him towards you."

"I'm sorry, ma'am? Hug him?" asked the Sergeant, a little taken aback.

"Yes, yes, hug him, cuddle him, embrace him. Whatever you like to call it. You've got to warm him up quickly but not too abruptly, otherwise his heart will stop."

"How long do I, erm, hug him for?"

"Don't move until he tells you to."

"When will that be?"

"When he's warmed up."

The Sergeant's military expertise meant that he automatically followed the most appropriate and effective procedure during times of emergency, subjugating everything to resolving the crisis. But taking orders of a somewhat questionable nature from a small, old woman, however sensible and correct he knew them to be, strained at his military pride. Deep inside him, the experienced army man quietly bristled with indignation.

"Help me with this, Thomas," said grandma pointing to the big pot. The young lad was there in an instant and together they lifted the heavy iron pot on to a blackened hook over-hanging the fire.

"Okay, now let's get to work on young Stanley here."

"Can I help?" Thomas bubbled.

"Go and heat up the stew in the kitchen. Our friends will be needing something hot to eat. It's in the pan on the stove, ready for tomorrow."

"Okay, grandma," he screeched and zipped away.

A charred and beaten kettle sat in the ashes of the fire. The old woman wrapped a cloth around her hand and poured the water from the kettle in to a wooden basin that sat next to the armchair. The basin was clearly the cut end of an old barrel and the smell of oak and ale wafted up in the steam. Carefully and tenderly she placed both Stanley's feet in to the warm water.

"Like blocks of ice," she mumbled. She looked up at the Sergeant. "We need to heat up the bits furthest from his heart or he'll lose them," she told him by way of explanation.

"How do we warm the heart up?"

"That's your job."

"Grandma?" came the shout from the busy sounding kitchen. "If we have our dinner now, what will we have tomorrow, for Christmas?"

"I'm sure the Lord will provide," she replied confidently.

The Sergeant began to speak, but she cut him off.

"He's dry now so hurry up and get all close and cuddly before he turns blue forever," she insisted.

The Sergeant did as he was told. He took off his coat, squeezed in to the armchair next to Stanley and wrapped his long arms around him.

"My God, he's absolutely freezing," exclaimed the Sergeant, somewhat alarmed.

The old woman patted the Sergeant on the thigh. "Then warm him up, Jock. Warm him up."

Stanley was still alternating between unconsciousness and delirium. His head lay lifelessly against the Sergeant's shoulder, his eyes half closed and his breathing laboured and shallow. Occasionally he would become agitated and garble a few unintelligible words, causing him to dribble out the corner of his numb mouth. A thin rivulet of spittle eventually spilled down his cheek and on to the Sergeant's arm. The Sergeant did not move. His embrace was strong and fired with paternal care. He did not realise how close to death Stanley was, and he'd seen far too much death for one lifetime. He wasn't prepared to see any more, and he wasn't ready to let Stanley shuffle soundlessly away in to the night like so many others of his boys. Although he knew it was probably too late, the Sergeant still held out hope of a child of his own one day, and if the Lord saw fit to bless him with a son, then he would protect him from the cruel ravages of life with all his strength and would not fail him like the other lads. Until then, he'd deal with Stanley; fatherless, guideless, alone, and very cold.

"Here are the others," sparked Thomas on seeing Martin and the old man come shivering through the cottage door. Both men were covered in tiny white icicles. The wind and rain screamed in from outside.

The woman looked up and smiled warmly. "Shut the door behind you, please. We're trying to reheat your friend."

Martin took in the scene.

"So I see," he said.

The house itself had been hard to see in the storm. In fact, it was not until they were less than fifty yards away that they realised the light they had been following was not the modern orange glow of a train station, but rather the roaring flames of a fire glowing in the hearth of an old and isolated stone cottage. The lack of any other source of illumination on the horizon meant that the firelight had blazed dramatically in the dark night and had pulled the men siren-like from their chosen path. The isolation also meant that getting a cab was probably not an option, Martin surmised. However, for now, he was pleased of the warmth. And anything to get rid of that donkey.

"How is he doing?" asked the old man caringly.

"He's warming up slowly."

"Did you put Rosa in the stable?" asked Thomas excitedly.

"Yes, she's all tucked up, nice and cosy, Thomas." replied the old man.

"Did you find her some hay?"

"Yes, she was munching away when we left."

"O good. I don't like to think of her being hungry. Thank you very much. How do you know my name?"

The quick fire, staccato nature of the young boy's speech seemed to catch the old man off guard.

"Erm, you told us earlier," he replied feebly. "After you saved our friend." The old man looked briefly at Martin, who wryly smiled.

"Rosa helped me. You see, grandma. I told you I saved the man. I don't remember telling you my name, though. Can we light the candles yet, grandma?" he asked without pausing.

In the corner of the living room, wedged between the little oak dining table and another smaller armchair, was the top of a small fir tree, freshly cut from the forest and smelling of pine. Its branches were decorated sparsely but thoughtfully with several home made stars carved skilfully from hazel wood and six antique-looking, beautiful, red glass baubles. On ten or so of its branches stood a thin white candle.

"Can we, grandma?" fizzed the young lad.

"Not yet, Thomas. You can see I'm busy at the moment." The old woman was kneeling on the floor bathing Stanley's feet and massaging his calves.

The young lad was visibly bursting with excitement, but the thrill of the evening was beginning to squeeze on his lungs. "O, please, grandma. It must be nearly time," he wheezed.

"Not yet. We need to deal with this gentleman first, and we need to feed our friends. Please calm down. There's a good boy. You'll only make yourself ill again."

"But it's getting late, grandma," he pleaded. "We have to light them before midnight." The young lad's breathing was becoming more rapid and shallow. His cheeks were turning pink.

"Then we've got another couple of hours yet, haven't we?" she said, pointing to the clock on the table. "Now please, Thomas, just relax. We can't have you getting ill now. Not now. We have to help poor Stanley here."

But it was too late. All this unanticipated excitement on Christmas Eve in such a loving and lonely boy proved too much for his sensitive airways and they collapsed inwards, clamping his chest. Panic shot across the young boy's innocent face.

"Thomas!" grandma cried, immediately recognising the signs.

In one movement, the old man leant forward and swept the boy up in to his arms.

"Come on, Thomas, listen to your grandma," he soothed, nodding reassuringly to the old woman and motioning for her to stay with Stanley. One of his large hands cradled the young lad, the other massaged the muscles around his neck. "Got to save some of your energies for Christmas tomorrow. Don't want to be too tired to open your presents, do you?"

The old woman looked on with grave concern. Why tonight of all nights, she asked herself. She could not ride to Dr Adler's in this storm. Besides, Rosa would be too tired and she had no money left for any medication. They still owed the doctor for the last lot.

"Anyway, we can't light the candles on the tree with you coughing and spluttering all over the place," the old man continued, his thick fingers gently kneading the boy's throat. "You'll blow them out."

Please let it pass, grandma silently prayed, please let it pass. She could not bear to see Thomas in such distress again, not after last time. Dr Adler said they had nearly lost him. She was up all night that time stroking his little head, watching helplessly as he gasped for air for hours on end, wishing above everything to be able to swap places.

"I was just like you when I was your age. Always getting over-excited, especially this time of year." The old man held Thomas close to his capacious chest and gently rocked him in time with his words. "My gran used to make me sit in a hot, steamy bath, close my eyes and drink warm sarsaparilla until all my muscles had gone soft." His deep, resonant voice dripped like honey over the young lad.

Grandma could not bear to watch any more. Even if he came through, it would still be an hour or so until his neck unshackled and his breathing slackened enough for him to smile. It was no good, she would have to brave the storm. Dr Adler could not deny them, surely. Not at Christmas. Poor little Thomas. Had he not suffered enough?

"Now how about we see how Rosa is getting on with that hay? See if we can find her a little treat or something." The old man took his hand off Thomas's neck and rummaged in his pockets. "I'm sure I've got something here. It's her Christmas as well, you know."

The young lad jumped down from the old man's arms.

"Can we, grandma?" he shouted, his voice beautifully clear and booming. "Can we go check on Rosa? She does get hungry."

The old woman stared in disbelief.

"Erm, yes. Yes, of course you can," she replied, her voice shaking with emotion. "Put your coat on," she added automatically. She removed her hands from the bowl and wiped her eyes. The warm water mixed with her tears and reddened her cheeks. She dabbed them with her sleeve. "Thank you," she silently mouthed to the old man. "Thank you so much."

The old man nodded and smiled.

"Ah, here we are," he declared to the young lad, pulling something out his jacket pocket. "I knew I had something in here for Rosa."

"You carry carrots in your pockets?" asked Martin incredulously.

"Always. Never know when they'll come in handy," he beamed. "Come on, Thomas. Wrap up well and let's give Rosa her well-earned Christmas present."

"She deserves it, doesn't she?" chirruped Thomas taking hold of the old man's hand and following him to the door.

"I should say so. Saving Stanley like that," he jollied.

As they faded in to the storm, Martin could just hear the old man say.

"Do you know, I think I might have an apple in here as well."

Within the hour Rosa had been fed and, after a long and stubborn battle, Thomas had finally surrendered to sleep. To everyone's relief,

Stanley had gradually regained consciousness and now sat in the large armchair tingling from head to toe. His movements were still sluggish and sore, but his skin was now a fiery, shiny crimson, as far removed as possible from the deathly, bluish hue the Sergeant knew so well and feared so much.

Stanley had finally woken twenty or so minutes earlier sitting in front of a baking fire of a strange house dressed in someone else's clothes. Any other day he would have panicked, but the night had so comprehensively removed the element of surprise from his life that he simply accepted it as the natural course of events. Besides, his body was so racked with fatigue and bruises, any course of action other than simple acquiescence would have been unthinkable.

He had very little memory of the past sixty minutes. He had a dim recollection of plummeting through the ice and of the sudden, breath stopping moment when his body hit the water, but remembered nothing after that apart from a sporadic awareness of being trapped in the strong and burning embrace of the Sergeant.

"How are you feeling?" asked the old woman softly, handing him a bowl of thick stew.

"Tired, but much better, thank you," he quietly replied. "Whose clothes are these?"

"My son's."

"Please pass on my gratitude to him."

"I will," replied the old woman somewhat sadly and returned to the kitchen.

The other three men sat cramped around the small oak table. The sounds of them tucking hungrily in to their food were interrupted only by the battering of the storm against the draughty leaded window. The Sergeant and the old man sat on two matching wooden stools, and Martin was perched on the side of the second armchair, trying not to disturb Thomas who was sound asleep on the comfortable old cushions.

Stanley looked down at his bowl. The stew steamed upwards and brought with it a familiar smell. Globules of golden goose fat sat in tiny puddles on the surface of the broth and oozed greasily around the thick chunks of potato and swede that made up the bulk of the dish. He poked his spoon tentatively in to the mixture as if inspecting it for clues and stirred it around two or three times. Lumps of white and brown meat floated to the top together with great swollen grains of barley and split peas bloated with gruel. Occasionally the bright orange of a carrot slice bobbed to the surface and interrupted the yellow melange.

"What is this?" he asked innocently.

The Sergeant wiped his mouth on his sleeve and looked at Stanley.

"It's their dinner," he said.

The stew was hearty and nutritious, Stanley was in no doubt. It was also cheap, cobbled together from leftovers and off-cuts, and reminded him painfully of his childhood. He looked in wonder at the enthusiasm with which the other three were devouring theirs.

"I'm not sure if I can eat it."

All three men stopped eating and looked at Stanley with a mixture of disbelief and disapproval. The Sergeant spoke first, his voice steady and insistent.

"Son, you're not only going to eat it, you're going to enjoy it, tell them how much you liked it, and thank them from the bottom of your heart for all their care and attention. This is their Christmas dinner they've insisted we eat, for God's sake. They'll probably go hungry tomorrow because of their stubborn generosity - a generosity, may I add, that you are only here to enjoy because the little lad saved your life."

"What do you mean 'the little lad' saved my life?"

"He's the one who pulled you out from under the ice," replied Martin. "Well, him and the donkey."

Stanley was genuinely shocked. "I thought … I assumed it was one of you."

"No, we were running around like headless chickens. We had no idea where you'd gone at first, and then when Jock realised you'd gone through the ice, all we could do was try to follow you."

"And pray," the Sergeant added.

"So, what happened?"

"Thomas appeared from nowhere. Out of the darkness, carrying his lamp, like a little angel, he was." The Sergeant's admiration for the young lad's conduct was clear. "Said he heard us shouting. Lucky we were upwind of him, although it's a miracle he heard anythin' in that storm, I can tell you."

"He was amazing," agreed Martin. "He quickly worked out where you were heading, kicked through the ice and then grabbed you as you went past. Him and the donkey pulled you up on a rope. Jock carried you back here. "

Stanley said nothing for a few moments. He sat, head bowed, staring vacantly at grandma and Thomas's Christmas dinner cupped in his lap. The steam from the bowl wreathed around his face and condensed in to delicate tear-like droplets on his cheeks.

His voice faltered. "But what was he doing out there at that time of night?" he asked.

"Collecting logs for the fire tomorrow," replied the Sergeant. "The wee lad is ten years old. He's out with his donkey on a freezin' night in a wicked storm. And still he comes to see if he can help a few indistinct voices swirlin' around in the dark."

Stanley's voice quivered with emotion. "He's ten years old? But - but why was …"

"Ten years old, nothing but rags to wear, but still better than any of us," the Sergeant interrupted. "And that's his dinner you're turning your nose up at. So, if you think you've *had enough* of it, already," the Sergeant scowled the words, "just be thankful that there's ten year old boys who don't give up as easily as you wandering around the night."

The Sergeant's words hit Stanley's weak and exhausted person with all the force of an axe, slicing through the last remaining vestiges of his once legendary self-assurance. He fell back in to his seat, emotionally shattered, and the guilt flooded in. All the certainties that had anchored Stanley throughout his young and turbulent life and had steadied his surge to business success while his contemporaries floundered around him, had somehow been hacked away in one single tempestuous evening. Sitting there in a tiny cottage, miles from home with only strangers for company, he felt cast adrift, unsure of where he was and no control over where the currents of fate would take him next. For the first time in years he was suddenly aware of how alone he was. He was lost and afraid. Unable to resist any longer, he began to cry.

The Sergeant was first to him. He stood over Stanley, awkward and reticent. The career soldier looked down and saw a poor young man trying to stifle his tears, and it was clear he had no idea what to do. Sheepishly he sat on the arm of the chair and squeezed Stanley's shoulder.

"Sorry, son" he managed. "Perhaps that was a bit harsh. Forgive me, it's been a long night." He hugged the young man momentarily towards him and Stanley's tear-stained face fell in to his shoulder. Unable to help himself, Stanley began to weep uncontrollably. The Sergeant, all sense of self-consciousness seemingly lost, bit his lip and held him tight. Stanley's despair crashed against his broad, bony chest like waves on a stony shore.

For a few minutes the room was quiet except for the rattle of the window and the muffled sounds of Stanley's tears. Martin and the old man sat in respectful silence waiting for the moment to pass. Eventually Stanley's anguish appeared to recede.

"I'm sorry," he choked, wiping his eyes on his sleeve. "I'm not sure what came over me."

"Don't worry, lad. These are trying times for all of us," said the Sergeant.

"Very true, Jock. Very true," grandma agreed. She had returned from the kitchen a few moments ago to see Stanley weeping on the big man's shoulder. "No point carrying the sadness by yourself, Stanley. S'good to let it out. The world can take it. It is heavy enough with grief this year."

"I really don't know why I'm so gloomy," Stanley sniffed. "I know I'm tired and it's been a punishing night, but at least I'm clean now, eh?! And my clothes have been washed." He nodded to his jacket and trousers steaming on a line hanging over the fire.

Everyone smiled.

"Sometimes, Stanley, life just catches up with you," said the old man meaningfully. "Especially when you're least expecting it."

"And especially at Christmas," Martin offered.

The old man lightly clasped Martin's arm.

"Okay, I think we could all do with a drink," announced the old woman. "A Christmas drink," she added, nodding at Martin. "I'll go and make some punch, and I expect a little bit of happy Christmas spirit when I return." She disappeared back in to the tiny kitchen and soon the heady smell of spices and fruit drifted in to the living room. The mood noticeably lifted.

"I've never had a happy Christmas," Stanley suddenly piped.

Even the old man seemed dumbfounded by this sudden public confession.

"Sorry, son?" asked the Sergeant

"A happy Christmas. I've never had one."

"Ach, come on," the Sergeant responded. "Everyone has. How about when you were a wee laddie?"

"No, I never have. Not one," Stanley reiterated. His voice was now calm and sincere. "I know you're supposed to love Christmas, especially as a child, but, well, I never did. Everyone talked about what a wonderful time it was, and how we were supposed to celebrate its true meaning and everything, but it never meant anything to me."

"What, nothing at all?" asked the old man.

"Nothing, you know, nice. If it meant anything it was other kids laughing at the rags the new boy wore to church, or their looks of pity on seeing me playing alone outside with my cheap toy; or sitting in some forgettable rented room listening to families either side of us feasting and making merry, while my mother and I sat in silence with a bowl of broth and a hunk of bread telling each other how lucky we were." He paused for a few moments and then, in the same composed tone, he continued. "It was, I suspect, a reminder of all the things we didn't have. No money, no friends. No father." He spoke without rancour and without a trace of his former reserve. It was as if his tears had unburdened him of his former aloofness and now he was spilling the contents of his soul. "Christmas," he stated, "it just seemed like life's way, once a year, of letting you know how much it had abandoned you. I suppose I've never forgiven it."

"It's about time you did then, Stanley," responded the old lady, entering the room with a jug of hot punch and four sparkling glass tumblers.

"You're an intelligent young man, Stanley, no doubt with the world at your feet, but that world will spin quite happily without you. Christmas is simply what you make it. You can celebrate it and rejoice in the good things it means and brings or you can sit around being miserable, cheating no-one but yourself. Believe me, the universe will be unaffected whatever you choose. But if you do have the chance to add to the general well of happiness in this life, and not everyone has, then it seems a pity to pass up such an opportunity. Lord knows, the world could do with some joy at the moment. Now I'm going to wake up Thomas so we can light the candles. He's had a tough year, the poor lad, so I'd appreciate it if we could lift some of the melancholy that, rather untraditionally, seems to have descended down the chimney over the last few minutes."

Stanley held Thomas high above his head so he could light the final candle. The little lad stretched his arm as far as he could, but it fell tantalisingly short.

"Higher, Mr Stanley," he urged. "I can't quite reach."

Stanley extended his shoulders and elbows to the end of their range. This was beginning to feel like hard work; little Thomas was heavier than he looked. Next year, he resolved, he would have to get fit.

"Higher," Thomas cried. The bright, yellow flame at the end of the lighter in Thomas's hand hovered barely an inch away from the candle's wick. "Nearly there," the boy grunted, his sinews at full stretch.

"Come on, Stanley. It'll be Twelfth Night soon," laughed the Sergeant.

Stanley's face was now bright red with effort. His head was aching and his arms were beginning to shake as the rigours of the past few hours started to take their toll.

"Please, just a bit higher," Thomas pleaded.

The cottage was suddenly feeling distinctly overheated. The living room was small and the fire burned fiercely. The back of Stanley's shirt tugged stickily on his back as he struggled to keep the boy aloft.

"Come on, Mr Stanley."

"Yes, come on Stanley," beamed Martin. "Some of us have homes to get to."

Stanley was actually feeling quite dizzy now. His head was pounding and the muscles around his shoulders throbbed with the strain. He didn't want to let the boy down, but he was actually feeling quite faint. His arms could stretch no further, so he stood on his toes, the lighter touched the wick and everyone cheered. Then he promptly keeled over backwards.

Everybody laughed, none more so than Thomas, who was in fits of giggles.

"Oh, it's so good to see him laughing again," whispered grandma to the Sergeant.

Stanley propped himself up on his arms, his blood pressure slowly returning to normal, and with mock nonchalance announced, "Nothing to it." Thomas jumped up and flung his arms joyfully around Stanley.

"Thank you, Mr Stanley. I hope you didn't hurt yourself."

Stanley thought of his aching limbs and the bruises thumping in his back. "Didn't feel a thing," he said.

Grandma squeezed the Sergeant's hand. "I know this sounds terrible and selfish," she quietly said, "but, now that Stanley's okay, I'm so glad you men happened by tonight. It's done Thomas the world of good."

The Sergeant nodded understandingly. "Aye, he's a wonderful lad. Brave as well."

The laughter gradually died down. Thomas sat on Stanley's outstretched legs, his face wreathed in smiles.

"Why haven't you got a father?" he suddenly asked.

"Pardon?" replied Stanley, somewhat taken aback.

"When you were talking earlier, you said you had no father," he innocently affirmed. "I heard you. I was awake on the chair." Thomas glanced over at his grandma. "Sorry, grandma."

"You were supposed to be asleep," said grandma, wagging her finger.

"Sadly, Thomas, my father died when I was young, very young."

"My father died also," he said matter-of-factly.

"Your father?"

"Yes, they're his clothes," he replied, nodding to Stanley's borrowed attire.

Stanley looked down at his shirt and then slowly up at Thomas. "I am very sorry to hear that. Very sorry, indeed." His sorrow for the young lad was deep and heartfelt. He thought of the photograph in his wallet. He hoped the water had not damaged it.

"He was killed in the war, wasn't he grandma?"

"Yes, he was, darling," she agreed. Thomas looked up at her with his big hazel eyes, smiling broadly. She leant forward and smoothed his brown tousled hair. "And you look just like he did when he was your age," she added, the sadness gathering in her smile.

Both Martin and Stanley blinked in confusion.

"How …" Stanley began to ask, but grandma cut him off.

"My, doesn't the tree look lovely," she declared, turning out the oil lamp which hung in the corner and wiping her eyes. She gently motioned to Stanley to change the subject.

Everyone dutifully looked at the tree, collectively trying to usher the moment past. But grandma was right, the tree did look beautiful. The candle flames flickered constantly in the draught from the window and sparkled against the red glass baubles that spun gently in the breeze. As they twisted they occasionally caught the candle light in such a way that a bright, momentary starburst dazzled the dark room, like the last gasp of a dying sun from a distant galaxy. It was like watching a twinkling night sky.

"Now that is a wonderful tree," confirmed the Sergeant.

Thomas stood up from Stanley's lap, walked over to his grandma and threw his arms around her waist.

"It is very pretty, grandma. Thank you for letting me stay up to light the candles."

The old woman squeezed him hard towards her.

"I'd like to make a toast," Stanley suddenly announced. "As you know, words are not exactly my strong point. Fortunately, that is of little import in this case, because words are not enough to express my appreciation for all that Thomas and grandma have done tonight." He looked at the old woman with an expression of deep gratitude. In strong and meaningful tones, he continued, "I want to thank you both from the bottom of my heart for all your help." He held his glass aloft. "A Merry Christmas to you."

Everyone raised their glasses.

"Yes, Merry Christmas, everyone," the old man cheered.

"Merry Christmas," echoed the Sergeant.

Martin nodded and drank his punch.

"Well said, Stanley," said the old man, patting him on the shoulder.

"Yep, well done, lad. Right thing to say, right time to say it," said the Sergeant.

"Can I open my present, please, grandma?" asked Thomas excitedly.

Beneath the tree were two presents: one wrapped in crepe paper and tied lovingly with a red ribbon; the other concealed behind a thick carapace of newspaper and string, as lovingly applied as the wrapping on the other gift, but with not such a skilful or mature hand. Attached to the first present was a piece of pink card on which was drawn a sprig of holly and a smiling snowman. Underneath the snowman, in delicate and careful handwriting were the words "To My Darling Thomas".

"If you open your present now, I will have nothing to give you tomorrow," replied grandma.

The old man sidled conspiratorially over to grandma. "Let him open his gift now," he encouraged. "You never know what tomorrow will bring." He beamed a knowing look at the old woman, which only served to confuse her.

Martin came to her aid.

"It doesn't matter what you think," he advised, "whatever he says, whatever he suggests, just go with it. It nearly always turns out to be true, even if it seems a bit weird at first."

The Sergeant and Stanley both laughed. The old man simply smiled.

To her apparent surprise she found herself saying, "Okay, Thomas, you can open your present now. It's nearly midnight anyway."

Martin checked his watch. It still read ten O'clock.

"O, thanks, grandma," called Thomas and dived under the tree to retrieve his present.

"He's a great boy, ma'am," said the Sergeant kindly. "A real credit to you."

"And to his father."

Thomas took his present over to the armchair by the fire and began to untie the ribbon. He clearly liked to take his time, to make the moment last.

"His mother died when he was a baby. Paul brought him up single-handedly."

"Sounds like a good man. I'm sorry for your loss."

"Thank you. We both miss him terribly."

Thomas was now carefully unpeeling the crepe paper.

"He hates tearing it," grandma said.

"Poor little lad, must be hard to lose your father at such a young age."

"Unthinkably hard," she quietly confirmed. "And hard to lose your son at any age."

"Aye, it must be." The Sergeant considered this for a moment. Such a small and loving family, yet such pain, he thought. "God damn this enemy," he cursed.

The old woman looked up at the Sergeant.

"Sergeant, forgive me, but I'll have no damning of anyone in this house. Not tonight, not any more. And especially when it's so misplaced."

The little lad had removed the crepe paper and folded it neatly in to a red concertina pile on the floor. As ever, the old woman had provided a second layer of wrapping; she also loved to make the moment last.

"Grandma!" shouted Thomas in mock indignation.

She smiled back.

"I'm – I'm sorry," the Sergeant stumbled. "No offence meant."

She patted him on the back of his hand. "And none taken," she assured. "Let's watch Thomas now."

The Sergeant stared at Thomas carefully untying the second ribbon.

"What do you mean "misplaced"?" he asked quietly.

Grandma sighed. "A man who's seen as much suffering as you, Jock? Surely you don't think the enemy are those other young men two hundred yards away across the mud? Paul used to say the only difference between us and them is that they're facing the other way."

"I'm sorry, I don't understand."

"They cry the same tears, bleed the same blood. They leave behind the same widows and orphans." She was whispering now, trying not to disturb Thomas's moment. "And the same bones rotting in the ground."

Thomas was nearly there; just a few more twists of the paper to unravel. His face practically swelled with anticipation.

"The enemy are not like us," the Sergeant rasped.

"Yes they are, they're exactly like us," grandma replied in hushed tones. "Human beings just trying to get by. They just happen speak another tongue, live in a different place."

"How can you say that, after what they have done to you and Thomas?"

"They? They've done nothing. They do the same to us as we do to them. There's only one enemy, Sergeant, and that's this war. This senseless, unforgivable loss of life. Such a terrible, terrible waste."

"I'm proud to serve my country, to pay my dues."

"My family have paid enough for their country, and we'll still be paying for it long after the governments have shaken hands and swapped business cards. Now please, my grandson's opening his Christmas present."

Thomas's eyes opened wide with unbridled delight.

"Grandma, it's fantastic," he cried and ran over to her, clutching the present to his chest. "O thank you," he said and kissed her wetly on the cheek.

"Do you like it?" she asked

"I do, I really do. Can I keep it by my bed?" She nodded. "Thank you. Mr Stanley, look what grandma has got me for Christmas," he shouted and then went to show his present to Stanley and the old man.

The Sergeant was struggling. The old woman's words had left him painfully confused. A large part of him agreed with her, but to admit that would be to deny all that he stood for, all that he believed. It was verging on treasonable to think that the horrors of this war were not the enemy's doing. As he always said, there was good and bad in this war, and they had to be on the side of good. You only had to look around at this family to see the agony the enemy had unleashed.

The old woman saw his discomfort. "Look, Jock," she said softly. "Don't get me wrong, I'm not a saint. If the man who killed my Paul were here now, I would struggle not to hate him and not to want to seek revenge for the hurt he's caused. But, tell me, would good would that do? The world is already overflowing with lonely widows and mothers mourning their sons."

"Look Mr Jock," said Thomas, pulling at the Sergeant's sleeve. "Look at my present." The little lad pushed in to his hand a small, oak-framed, black and white photograph. It was of Thomas sitting on the shoulders of a handsome man in his army uniform. They were both smiling broadly. "It's my father," Thomas said proudly.

The Sergeant looked down at the photograph. There was Thomas laughing with unconfined glee at the camera, clearly revelling in his father's company; and there was his father, looking smart in his neat grey uniform, a beaming smile and a large dark moustache spread across his face, which the Sergeant immediately recognised as that of the German soldier he had killed earlier that evening.

19.
HOME

The sounds of the Sergeant's wailing could be heard for miles. His screams, almost bestial in their anguish, ploughed through the storm and echoed out across the frozen lake and in to the woods beyond. In the darkness they merged seamlessly with the howls of a nearby wolfpack, and in his distressed state the Sergeant knew that these were not simple creatures of the forest, but the hungry the wolves of Time, tracking down the minutes of his life with tireless certainty. Relentless and determined, he could feel them gaining on him with every minute. Somewhere a clock struck midnight and he realised with an unshakeable and dreadful conviction that they were closing in for the kill.

He had run from the cottage as soon as the enormity of his crime became apparent, but his legs had soon buckled under the weight of his shame, and he now sat on the ice, barely yards from the house, utterly overwhelmed with despair. It was he who had robbed Thomas of a father, his hand that had taken the old woman's son. Killed not in the wrath of battle, or by the terrible lottery of the sniper's bullet, but murdered in cold blood, defenceless and alone in a foreign trench.

Inside the cottage the situation was confused. The Sergeant's sudden departure had initially been met with a stunned silence.

Thomas picked up the photograph, mercifully undamaged, and looked at his grandma. He tried hard to resist, but eventually his bottom lip begun to tremble.

"It's okay, Thomas, no damage done," she soothed, stroking his head. She looked at the men. "Surely someone needs to go after him? The ice is not a place to be alone with your demons."

"I'll go," said Stanley immediately.

He went to rise from his stool but was gently restrained by the old man's hand. A thick mist was pouring through the open door from the storm outside, blown in on the droning, squalling wind. It swirled around the room and rapidly filled all the corners and crannies of the tiny cottage. And as the mist swirled, so the wind hummed and moaned, gusting in deep, regular beats, as if in concert with the midnight chimes ringing from the clock on the table.

"Time to go, gentlemen," said the old man.

Stanley looked over at Thomas and the old woman. They were hard to see in the fog, no more than dim outlines. He was surprised to see they were chatting amiably, seemingly unaware of the dense mist or of the presence of the men.

"What on Earth …?" said Stanley.

"Stanley, I know this is a bit confusing."

"That's an understatement."

"And I know it's been a difficult night for you, but please trust me, we need to go."

Stanley remained unmoved.

"I'm not going anywhere until someone explains what's going on." He looked around at the enveloping mist. "This … this is your doing?"

"No. Not really."

"So what's happening then? Am I dreaming? Am I insane?"

"No, this is real," the old man assured him.

"Everything here is real, is it? We're here, in this cottage, miles from anywhere? "

"Yes." The old man hesitated for a moment. "Well, sort of. Look Stanley, we're all just a product of circumstance, and while the circumstances may change, the feelings you have, the decisions you make, they're what's important, they are what's real."

"It's a strange old reality, as far as I can see," he barked. Then more softly, "So the mist at Frank's house and everything, that really happened?"

The old man nodded. Stanley seemed a little relieved.

"And the crash and the ice – you did all that?"

"No, not at all," the old man bristled. "The night unfolded as you made it. I'm just here to help."

Stanley gazed bewildered around the room.

"Believe me, Stanley, everything will be explained soon, but for now, gentlemen, please...." The old man motioned to the door.

There was a moment's quiet as both Stanley and Martin gathered their thoughts.

"Where to?" asked Martin.

"We need to take Jock home."

Martin nodded and walked to the cottage door, outwardly calm. A nervous twitch tugged at his face. "I think I've worked it out," he whispered to the old man as he went past.

Stanley continued to gape at the dim images of the old woman and her son.

"I know it's difficult, but we do need to leave, Stanley. Contrary to appearances, time is not our friend."

"But.."

"Please, Stanley"

Stanley stared at the faint silhouettes across the room. Things were clearer now.

"Will they remember us?" he asked.

"In a way."

"What does that mean?"

"More than a dream. Less than a memory," the old man replied gently.

"I would have liked to have given them something," said Stanley regretfully.

"There will be other Christmases, other opportunities."

Stanley followed the old man apprehensively to the door. As he passed the wispy figures of Thomas and grandma he looked down with some sadness.

"Thank you," he quietly said.

"Frohe Weihnachten, Grosmutti," replied Thomas, although his words were barely audible through the fog and pulsing wind.

"Frohe Weihnachten, meine darlinke Enkel," said the old woman. "Am Weihnachtsbaum die Lichter brennen

But he wasn't sure if they were talking to him.

Martin was the first out of the door. To his great surprise, it was exactly as he expected. An icy storm and a biting wind, just as he'd left it. Except for one thing. On the edge of the frozen lake stood Jock, his eyes scarlet with tears, staring straight ahead. A dense bank of mist blew vortex-like around him, but he did not notice; he continued to look intently forwards at what the fog had brought him.

"That's a relief," said Stanley, suddenly appearing next to Martin. "I was a bit, well, you know. Didn't know what to expect." Then he saw the Sergeant. "Oh," he managed.

The old man walked past them and in to the huge, twisting eddy of mist that circled around the Sergeant. The cloud rapidly grew outwards, swirling as it did so, until Martin and Stanley were caught in the thick, dry haze. Stanley looked back to see if the cottage had been claimed by the fog, but it was gone.

The old man placed his hand kindly on the Sergeant's shoulder. He did not move.

"Is it too late, Mel?" he said, still staring forwards.

"Too late for what?"

"Forgiveness."

"Forgiveness for whom?"

The Sergeant turned and looked uncomprehendingly at the old man. His eyes were swollen and red, his hair sticky with tension.

The old man relented. "Forgiveness is not a matter of time," he said kindly.

"I need to go home."

"I know, Jock. I know."

"But I don't know why. Do you?" he asked firmly.

The old man sighed to himself and shrugged in as non-committal way as he could manage. The Sergeant turned his gaze once more forwards.

"You make a terrible liar, Mel," he joked. "Never go to war."

The old man smiled sadly. He motioned for Martin and Stanley to join them.

The Sergeant focused once again on the sight in front of him. In the bank of mist straight ahead was a large wooden door. It was set in a bluff stone archway housed in a red brick wall, and although the masonry fixtures drifted in and out focus as the cloud spun and swelled, the door itself always remained clear. Sometimes it was possible to make out a large part of the face of the building it served; other times, when the wind gusted hard, it appeared as if the door existed in isolation, hovering by itself in the fog like some ghostly architectural apparition. But the door was real. It was made of dark wood, now somewhat weathered, and had a solidity about it that spoke of industry and craftsmanship. A big, black metal handle, worn smooth from use and lifted slightly away from the wood, sat on its right side and in the middle was a small grilled window fitted with smoked glass. Underneath the window, carved deep in to the oak, was the word 'INFIRMARY'.

"I assume this is the way," stated the Sergeant, trying to suppress the sense of foreboding rising within him.

"Yes," agreed the old man. "But we will just be visitors. It will not be like here. We'll be onlookers only."

"Sights to see, but nothing to do, eh? Sounds like my life, alright." The Sergeant closed his eyes and slowly exhaled. "Time to go home," he said. He stepped forward, pulled firmly on the handle and walked through the door and out of the fog.

A short distance away, out in the moonlit darkness, the howling stopped.

They were in a corridor. A long, poorly lit and empty corridor. The floor was tiled and the hollow sounds of the men's footsteps tapped noisily in the silence. Windows dotted one side, each one decorated with cheap tinsel and paper chains which looped lazily from corner to corner. Here and there a small plant sat in a terracotta pot on the sill. Most were dusty with cobwebs and as dry as tinder, but all somehow clung to life. In one of them, someone had poked a small sprig of holly in to the arid soil, as if the verdant, evergreen leaves and bright red berries would rejuvenate the ailing plant.

Along the other side of the corridor ran a series of doors. The old man stopped at the penultimate one.

"We're here."

"This isn't home," said the Sergeant defiantly.

"This is where you need to be," the old man softly replied.

The Sergeant looked down at his hands. His palms were sweating, so he wiped them on his trousers. He had been afraid before, of course; been afraid many times, in fact. But he had never had such an overpowering feeling of dread. He supposed this was natural. A man does not usually have notice of his destiny. He pushed through the door.

Beyond was a medical suite in which two doctors and two nurses busied around a prostrate patient. He could not see the patient, but he didn't have to. In his heart he knew who the patient was. There was clearly some sort of medical emergency in process judging by the frantic shouts of the hospital staff to each other. He could not hear exactly what was being said or see precisely what was going on, as everything appeared somehow muted. It was like watching a play through a crack in the door and reminded him of when he used to sneak in to the local playhouse as a kid and secretly watch the touring theatre groups act out their strange dramas. Except this time he knew the ending.

"Remember, they cannot see or hear us," advised the old man.

"Why have I been brought here?" asked the Sergeant. "There must be a reason. I know I've not been an entirely good man, not led a pure life, but there have been many worse." His despair was now infusing with anger as his time fell away. "Why me? A man should not be witness to his own demise."

The Sergeant ran his hands through his hair and pushed his fingers roughly in to his forehead, trying desperately to come to terms with a situation beyond the realms of reason. In the background the medical emergency was seemingly coming to a head. One doctor stood at the level of the patient's abdomen and barked orders to the other staff positioned at both ends of the table. The whole ghastly scene was drawing inexorably to its inevitable and terrible conclusion, the Sergeant realised. It was a pity, there were still so many things he'd planned to do: buy that blasted smallholding; drive a car; tell his wife how much he loved her. And he would have loved to have a child, to be a father.

With awful finality, the Sergeant found himself performing an audit of his dashed hopes and unfulfilled dreams, and as he did so, the anger and despair left him and were replaced by a profound and overwhelming sadness.

The doctor shouted more orders, and movements became more urgent and instructions more animated. The Sergeant steeled himself for the darkness to come. He wondered if it would be busy and full of sound or whether he would go mad in the silence. He felt the old man squeeze his arm, offering him support. The medical team were now yelling at each other. This was it. The Sergeant closed his eyes and waited for the cold rush of oblivion. The doctor's calls grew louder and louder, and clearer and clearer, until, with a jolt, they became the sound of a baby crying.

"It's a boy, Mrs Craig," said the midwife, taking the baby from the doctor. "A beautiful, bouncing, healthy boy." She cleaned the baby with a skill and speed honed from three decades of deliveries, and placed the squashed and battered new-born on the chest of the Sergeant's wife.

"You did well, Mrs Craig," said the senior doctor. "Lost a bit of blood, but you'll soon recover. May be a little sore for a while."

The Sergeant opened his eyes.

"What?!" he murmured, terrifyingly confused. "I don't underst…"

He stood staring incredulously at the scene unfolding in front of him, utterly unable to cope with the sudden emotional transition.

"What?" he finally demanded, reluctant to release his feelings until he had confirmation of what he had seen. "A child?! A son? Do I have a son, Mel?" he gasped.

"Yes, Jock," replied the old man, rather sombrely. "You have a son. Congratulations."

The Sergeant was silent for a few moments. He gazed at the floor, breathing loudly and rapidly, trying to manage the volcanic happiness that was building inside; he was afraid it would erupt uncontrollably and with such force that something of this moment would be lost forever.

He lifted his head. "Boys," he whispered reverentially to Martin and Stanley who were standing at the back of the room watching. "I have a son."

They both smiled, Martin more so. Stanley appeared a little unsettled by the situation.

"I have a son," the Sergeant repeated more loudly and to no-one in particular.

The adrenalin still cascaded through his veins in preparation for his imminent death and it now heightened the pure, visceral delight he felt to almost delirious levels. His heart was beating so fast he was scared it would burst from his chest. From the depths of sorrow to the giddy peaks of joy in one bellowing, baby's cry; it was, quite literally, a breathtaking way to travel.

The Sergeant walked over to the bed. The doctors and nurses were still fussing around his wife, making her comfortable and treating her wounds, but while they cleaned and sewed and dressed, she sat propped up on three pillows gaping lovingly down at her baby, oblivious of their ministrations. He'd forgotten how tough his wife could be; he knew all that attention must leave its mark. He felt a sudden rush of love for her that washed through him with such intoxicating force he was momentarily taken back to the Shanghai opium den his corporal had dragged him to as a newly enlisted teenager. Just like then, he felt almost sick on the dizzying pleasures of this new drug.

How he wished he could hold her. How he yearned to hold them both. He couldn't see his son properly, but the love he felt for that tiny, blood-stained, bruised and beautiful figure nestling in his mother's arms was immediate and all-embracing.

"It's a fantastic feeling, isn't it?" said Martin, appearing next to him. "I remember when Chris was born," he added wistfully. Stanley and the old man kept a respectful distance, but Martin seemed to feel compelled to share in the moment with the Sergeant. "He's absolutely gorgeous, Jock. I'm really pleased for you."

"Thanks, Martin," he replied warmly without taking his eyes of his son.

"You're going to make a great father."

"Do you think so?"

"Absolutely."

And at that moment the Sergeant knew Martin was right; he would be a great father, the world's best. He reckoned he'd seen most of the evils on God's Earth and the first lesson they taught you in training was to know your enemy. He would be his son's guide and protector, leading him safely through the cruel minefield that this life set before all young men. Sergeant Fraser Craig, the man who had seen such sadness and such pain, who had witnessed the worst depths of the human condition, vowed at this, the happiest point of his life, to be the greatest father the world had ever seen; the father he'd never had, the father he never thought he would be. His joy was indescribable and unbounded, and he wanted to share it with the whole human race.

"Why didn't you tell me, Mel?" he sang, gaze still firmly fixed on his son. "Why did you let me think I was going to die, you daft old fool?" he laughed.

The Sergeant looked up, but time had already moved on.

"I want to take him to see his dad," said the Sergeant's wife.

She looked different. Less bedraggled, but still tired. Her hair had been combed and her nightclothes changed. It was almost forty-eight hours since the baby's birth.

"I'm afraid that's out of the question," the doctor replied. "You've lost some blood and you'll be too weak to walk for a few days."

"Then I'll take a chair. Nothin' wrong with my arms."

"Mrs Craig, your stitches are fresh. Sitting down on anything will be extremely sore."

"After what I've been through over the past forty-eight hours, a little bit of soreness will come as a relief. Now, it's still Christmas Time, just, and I want to take my son to see his dad. He only came off the boat tonight."

"I'm sorry, but no."

"Doctor, it's very late, we're both tired and I appreciate you've got my best interests at heart, but take it from me, my son is goin' to see his dad tonight, even if I have to drag him there in my nightdress."

"I'll get you a chair," said the doctor, accepting the futility of further argument.

The Sergeant swelled with pride watching his wife. He'd never seen her like this, as others see her. Presumably, he was staying at a local hotel, or somewhere in the hospital, and wasn't due to see his wife until tomorrow. He was touched that his wife could not wait until morning. She would know how desperate he would be to see them both. Strange they shipped him back to see his child.

The doctor returned with a wheelchair.

"Would you like me to ask one of the nurses to go with you?"

"No, we'll be fine. Besides, I'd like to keep it private."

The Sergeant looked on in wonder as she wrapped their son tightly in a blanket, pulled her dressing gown roughly around her and struggled in to the chair. She placed the baby firmly and snugly in her lap and set off along the corridor, the Sergeant and the other men close behind. When she was out of sight of the doctor, she half stood on the chair and rearranged her gown to provide something a little softer to sit on.

"Should have brought a pillow," she muttered to herself, but then looked down at her baby son and added more brightly, "But didn't want to keep your daddy waiting, did I?"

The baby's face poked out of the blanket. The bruising from his delivery had eased and he looked impossibly pink. She bent down and kissed him softly on the forehead.

"Wait till he sees you, eh?" she hushed. For a few moments she seemed almost sad, but then breezily continued on her way.

"Take it slowly, love," urged the Sergeant when he saw that wheeling the chair was a bit more of a strain than she'd anticipated. After thirty or so yards she stopped, clearly in some discomfort, and rubbed her belly. The Sergeant spoke as if they were in the same room. "Perhaps the doctor was right. Perhaps it is too early to be doing stuff like this." He was starting to feel a little guilty about his wife going through this on his behalf. "I'm sure I can wait till morning."

"Can't stop now, can I darling?" she said, setting off once again. "Daddy's waited so long for you. It's not right to keep him waiting."

The Sergeant choked back the tears. Part of him felt uncomfortable intruding on his wife's private thoughts, another part wanted to shout to the world and let it know how much his wife loved him. They were now a family, a proper family. He could not wait to be together.

She turned in to a darker part of the corridor.

"Nearly there, sweetheart," she trilled.

This part of the building was older than the rest. It was cold with no windows and only the occasional lamp to light the way. The floor was made of stone, which was grooved and worn with use, and the chair's wheels squeaked as they rolled across the cool ashen surface. It puzzled the Sergeant as to why he would be staying down here. Saving money, probably. A Sergeant's wage would struggle to cover a new family and a hotel. That was something he would have to think about.

The baby cried out. In unison, the Sergeant and his wife looked down from their different worlds with sudden concern at the tiny boy. Wrapped tightly in his warm blanket, he was becoming restless as the winter air buffeted his sensitive little face.

"I'm sorry, darling," said the wife regretfully. "I know it's cold and late, but I have to tell your daddy something. Anyway, we're here now."

She turned the chair through a set of double doors in to a darkened anteroom. Along the sides of the room were two tables covered with white muslin. On one was an aged Nativity scene, complete with shepherds, Magi and an entire menagerie of farm animals. It had clearly been set out with great care, although the paint was peeling from many of the models and a couple of the goats seemed to have lost a leg, one of them knocking over the figure of Mary. Either side of the scene were two thick, white candles, their flames casting a flickering amber light over the First Christmas. The Sergeant's wife reached out and placed Mary's figure back on her feet.

"From one new mother to another," she said rather sombrely.

The other table was empty apart from a small wooden cross and a holly wreath sitting propped up against the wall at the end. They looked a little lost on such a large table, as if left behind by guests hurrying home for Christmas.

At the end of the anteroom were two more doors set with glass and draped with thick, velvet curtains. The Sergeant had seen this done in the trenches; bulky sheets of black carpet hung up over dug-out entrances to absorb the noise and light. They worked superbly, so much so that they were eventually banned as they were causing the exhausted men to over-sleep. Personally, he never liked them. Since Ypres, he had not been a lover of silence.

His wife pushed her way through the double doors. The Sergeant followed a little way behind. Although it would be a bit strange, he couldn't wait to see the look on his face when he saw his son. It would be like being dragged from the grave and given another life, like feeling the sun on his face after an endless, colourless winter. What a thrill to have something to look forward to at last.

And then he saw himself.

"Jock, love, this is your son," said his wife, rising shakily from the chair and holding up the baby. "Isn't he beautiful? He's everythin' we ever wished for. Everythin' you ever dreamed. I never told you before, because I didn't want to worry you. He was born two days ago, just after you ..." She began to cry. "I had to bring him to meet his daddy. I knew you'd want to see him straight away. You've dreamt of this for so long."

She broke down.

The Sergeant turned round to see the other men shuffling through the door.

"No, no, tell me it's not true," he screamed. "Tell me this is not how it ends."

"I'm sorry, Jock," said the old man.

"How can you do this to me? This is not fair, it's not right. You cannot torment a man like this."

"This is your life, Jock."

"How? How is this my *life*?" he spat. He pointed to the corpse which lay serenely on the chapel table, covered in white cotton and surrounded by candles. His wife sat head bowed in the chair holding the Sergeant's cold hand, completely overcome with grief. She hugged her baby son tightly towards her in a vain effort to provide some comfort.

"You were shot on Christmas Eve," explained the old man.

"Christmas Eve? I can't have been. No-one was shooting at anyone."

"You were shot by your own subaltern."

"What?!"

"He saw you were going to execute the German soldier."

TONY WILSON

"The old woman's son?"

"Yes."

"So I didn't kill him?"

"No, he died later in a prisoner of war camp."

The relief he felt at this news was immediately swamped by a more appalling realisation.

"I was shot by own side? I die a traitor?!" the Sergeant howled. "After all these years serving my country?!" He turned to his wife and son. "I'm sorry, darling, I'm so sorry."

Martin and Stanley stood at the back of the room struggling to deal with such raw emotion. Stanley openly wept.

The Sergeant's wife wiped her eyes with a small, cotton handkerchief. "I know you can't hear me, love, but I just wanted... needed to tell you how much better my life has been for meetin' you. I know I never told you, properly told you, and now I never will ..." she swallowed, "but I love you so much. I always will. We always will." The grief was too much to bear and she broke down again.

"Why bring me here, Mel?" cried the Sergeant. "Why torture me with these images? What's the point of this night, if there's no dawn to follow?

"To show you how each life affects all those it brushes against."

"Is it not enough that my son grows up without a father, my wife without a husband?"

"This is how your life plays out based on the choices you've made."

"The choices I've made?"

The old man nodded sadly.

The Sergeant stood panting, raging with anger and despair.

"Well, I choose life, do you hear me? I choose life. I choose fatherhood, I choose family, I choose humankind. I - I choose forgiveness," he swept his arm wildly out in front of him, "for every

182

man on the planet. Do you hear me? I choose them all, but what's the point if the grave has already claimed me. What's the point if they are choices I can no longer make?"

He collapsed under the surge of his lament. The weight of his anguish and desolation were unbearable, and he rested his head against the cold metal of the chapel table and waited for Death to find him. He was still crouching in this position when a ball hit him hit square in the face.

20.
HOME FRONT

"Oops, sorry Sarge," said Private Harris.

"Come on, Sarge, if you're going to play, at least make the effort," shouted Corporal Brayden. "We're 2-1 down."

"Glad you changed your mind," said the cook, picking the Sergeant up off the frozen pitch. "Although, you could have headed that a bit better," he laughed. "Happy Christmas, Sarge," he said and run off after the ball, far across the solid mud of no man's land.

The Sergeant stood with difficulty. He was shaking and utterly disorientated. The surroundings appeared hazily familiar, and he squinted disbelievingly at them, his eyes struggling to focus. Slowly, he raised his hand to his face where the football had hit. It was sore. The cold night air wafted against his cheeks, intensifying the sting. Warily, he turned his head side to side, trying to survey the scene, but unsure and unwilling to trust what he was seeing. He crouched down and scratched at the ground, and felt the cold, spiky earth under his fingers, and gasped. Breathing rapidly now, he turned his hands and looked at his palms; they were no longer trembling.

He was back! And he wasn't dead! O dear God, thank you, thank you so much! The happiness coursed through him like tidal swell. It washed away the pain that for so long had beached on his soul and brought with it the fresh, bright promise of a new land, a new life. Good old, Mel, he thought. Somehow from his sack of surprises, he had gifted him that most precious of Christmas presents, Time. He raised his hands to the starry heavens and shouted "Yes!" at the top of his voice.

At which point the ball landed at his feet.

The younger cook sprinted down the wing. "Pass it back, Sarge," he called.

"On my 'ead," advised the aged Corporal Percival, who had taken up a somewhat optimistic position twenty yards from the two flaming oil drums that served as goalposts.

But the Sergeant was on his way. With a skill that surprised everyone, he ran across the pitch, laughing as he went, controlling the ball across the icy earth with a dexterity that belied his years, and hobnail boots. He swerved this way and sidestepped that way, rounding the opposition players with a silky ease and uncanny speed, fuelled simply by the pure joy of being alive. After refusing all increasingly desperate invitations to pass the ball, he finally found himself with a clear shot on goal.

"Have a shot, Sarge," urged the cook.

"On my 'ead," pleaded Corporal Percival.

With a quick glance at the heavens, the Sergeant drew back his foot and, seconds before two burly German defenders arrived to tackle the cockiness out of him, he hoofed the ball as hard as he could way beyond and wide of the goal.

"Oh," managed a surprised Private Harris.

Corporal Percival stomped back to the half way line, his one chance of glory having disappeared in to the frozen night.

"Sorry, lads," the Sergeant said, trying hard not to smile. "I'll get it," and promptly ran off giggling in to the darkness. Behind him, rapidly fading in to the wintry air, he heard the puzzled discussions of his team-mates.

"That's the worse shot I've ever seen."

"Still, at least the miserable sod has cheered up."

"I s'pose we better ask them for another ball."

The ball bounced and bounced on the frozen mud until finally rolling to a halt on the outer reaches of no-man's land. The Sergeant followed it like an enthusiastic schoolboy, his breath freezing in a mist around his beaming face. He picked up the ball and scanned the darkness until he found him. The sight of the German soldier dragging himself across the rutted earth was both a relief and a sadness. The Sergeant crunched slowly over to the forlorn figure, crouched down and gently tapped him on the shoulder.

"Mein Freund, Paul," he said kindly.

The soldier craned his neck upwards, a confused and pained expression on his face. Blood oozed thickly from his ears.

"I'm going to help you," mimed the Sergeant, smiling. He then set about piling up sandbags for the German to rest against, all the time gesticulating wildly. "And then I'm going to take you back to yer own. Away from any camp."

For a while the soldier squinted at the Sergeant with a mixture of alarm and bewilderment, unable to comprehend this strange man and his animated gestures. However, it soon became apparent that the Sergeant's grinning features and feverish hand motions were clearly not those of an enemy combatant and relief visibly flooded the disorientated German. A thin smile broke out across his grimy face as he sank gratefully in to the dirt of no-man's land. The Sergeant, compensating for his linguistic limitations with ever more pronounced signals with his arms, gently pulled the exhausted soldier on to his back and sat him up against the mound of sandbags. He then cleaned the soldier's face with the sleeve of his shirt and handed him a cap of drink from his hip flask. The parched German swallowed it in one gulp.

"Be careful with that, friend," laughed the Sergeant, "that's ten year old single malt."

"Sehr gut," coughed the soldier. "Sehr gut," he spluttered at the top of his voice, his ears still buzzing and useless.

Chuckling, the Sergeant poured another cap of drink for them both.

"Not so quickly this time," he gestured, but the soldier's eyes had settled on the football bouncing on the Sergeant's leg. He stared at it in the darkness with complete bemusement.

"Ach, don't mind that," said the Sergeant, "I think you're winning anyway."

And there they sat under a sparkling winter's sky, the Sergeant and a thoroughly confused German sharing a Christmas drink together.

The Sergeant looked at his watch - it was midnight. He raised his drink.

"Frohe Weihnachten, Paul," he said.

"Frohe Weihnachten....erm?" replied the soldier, seeking his comrade's name.

"Jock."

"Jock," he nodded.

On seeing the soldier's puzzled look at the strange sounding name, the Sergeant patted him on the hand and grinned.

"Don't worry, Paul," he said reassuringly. "Everything is going to be alright."

Never had he meant something so much in all his life.

21.
STANLEY'S RETURN

The mist had returned.

It swirled around the three men as they walked slowly along the familiar cobbled street that had materialized out of the fading ghost of the hospital chapel. All three were silent. Stanley fumbled for something in his wallet.

"Just so I can be sure," he said uncertainly to the old man, his voice puncturing the still night air. "He is *not* now killed in the war?"

The old man looked caringly at Stanley. "It is not for us to guess Jock's actions or the consequences of those actions," he replied. On seeing Stanley's pleading look, he added, "But, yes, he has been given the opportunity to make a different choice."

Stanley unfolded the photograph in his hand. It was of a young man, about Stanley's age, broad and upright, grinning at the camera.

"And if he doesn't get killed in the war, then ...," he hesitated for a moment as if nervous of getting something wrong, " ... that will have an effect on all those his life subsequently touches?" he affirmed, remembering the old man's words in the chapel.

"Yes, that's true."

Stanley looked down at the worn and creased picture of the Sergeant.

"Then I will have a father," he whispered.

It was not asked as a question and so merited no reply. Instead, the men simply continued to shuffle along the cobbles, each alone with their thoughts. After a few minutes the old man stopped.

"We're here, Stanley," he said, motioning to the big house covered in white lights that had now appeared out of the fog.

Stanley half smiled. "I don't know if I've got enough energy for a party now."

"Nonsense. Christmas Eve? A young man like you?" jollied the old man. "Anyway, Frank's expecting you."

"I'm a little late."

"You always are."

Stanley turned to Martin and warmly shook his hand. "Thank you, Martin. I'm sorry for being so useless back at the train and everything."

"Don't worry about it. Something tells me it was all a part of Mel's master plan anyway, so you probably had no choice."

"I doubt that very much," Stanley replied.

"I hope it all works out for you," said Martin sincerely. He then added, "At least you get to taste some more of that punch."

Stanley smiled and turned back to the old man.

"So, do we get an explanation?" he asked kindly. "You did promise."

"Is there one that would satisfy you?"

"I'm not sure. The truth would be a start."

"May be a bit difficult."

"I suspected as much," confirmed Stanley, "but try anyway. After tonight, I think I'll be able to cope with most things."

"What is it you want to know?"

"O, Mel," said Stanley, "Just tell us why we're here."

"Very well, I'll do my best." The old man stroked his beard and coughed lightly, clearing his throat. He began, "There are some things…."

Stanley interrupted, "And if you could make it as clear and simple and as grounded in reality as possible, that would be helpful. Not so much of the enigmatic stuff, if you take my meaning. This is the 1930s after all." He nodded to Martin, "Present company excepted."

The old man tittered and his large, watery eyes looked upon Stanley with obvious affection. "Glad to see you haven't lost any of your negotiating skills," he chortled. "I knew tonight would be difficult." He said nothing for a short while, then beamed at the two men and heaved an enormous sigh. "Gentlemen, all I know is that sometimes, for reasons I don't understand, people get the opportunity for a second chance, to turn another corner, as it were."

The old man paused.

"And?" encouraged Stanley.

"And it's my responsibility, my privilege, to help them to their particular crossroads. Which road they take, what decision they make, that's down to them. I'm just a guide."

The two men thought about this for a few moments.

"Why at Christmas?" asked Stanley.

"Can you think of a better time of year?" the old man gleamed. "Or a better gift than a second chance?"

Stanley smiled warmly. "I take your point."

"Besides, forgiveness, hope, charity, they're all part of the Christmas Message," the old man added.

Martin tapped his shoes on the shiny cobbles, his face impassive. For a short while the patter of his heels was the only sound.

"So, who are you, Mel?" asked Stanley. "Who are you really?

"I'm just a normal man, like you," he claimed.

"Forgive me, but I don't think so."

He continued, "But one who has been lucky enough to have been given a special…," he pondered for a moment, "… position in life. I've been around a little longer, as well."

"So what does that make you?" asked Stanley, doggedly chasing the point. "Some kind of spirit?"

The old man chuckled. "A spirit? Me?!" He patted his bulging waistline. "I'm far too real."

"A dream?" offered Martin.

"Too alive."

"A ghost?" mocked Stanley

"Not scary enough."

"The tooth fairy," declared Martin.

"And now we're just being silly."

They all laughed. It was the laughter that precedes an imminent parting and it reluctantly petered out in to an edgy silence. Stanley looked down once more at the picture of the Sergeant.

"Time to go, Stanley," the old man said.

"Will he be there?"

"That's his choice."

"But what do I say? How do I react?"

"As you always have."

Carefully, Stanley refolded the photograph and placed it back in his wallet.

"Thank you, Mel," he said, and after a moment's awkward hesitation borne of a lifetime without practise, he stepped forward and embraced the old man. He then walked up the path towards the house. He had only gone a few yards when he stopped and called back,

"More than a dream, less than a memory?"

The old man nodded, and then both he and Martin watched as Stanley walked through the door and the house slowly disappeared in to the mist.

Many years later, Stanley Craig, successful co-founder of The Franstan Co-operative Group, was asked for his opinion by the eldest of his three daughters as to what to call her forthcoming child. She had been arguing with her husband for months about the baby's name and they both thought that he might able to help them with some impartial advice. After all, his arbitration skills were legendary in the industry, although he had never lost the flinty negotiation talents inherited from his father. As with all matters relating to family, Stanley listened carefully and spoke from the heart, another of his father's traits, and his daughter and son-in-law were pleased with the name he suggested, although Stanley appeared to be at a loss as to why the name so readily came to mind. And so it was on Christmas Day four months later that Stanley's first grandchild, Martin, was born.

22.
NOWHERE

"So what happens now?" asked Martin.

"That's up to you."

"Choices again, eh?"

"I suppose so."

Martin looked around him. They were, well, nowhere. He could see the cobbles under his feet and could plainly see the old man, but that was about it. Everywhere else was thick with mist. He assumed he was supposed to think he was in some kind of otherworldly waiting room, hanging around for the conclusion of his story.

"The thing is, I have a problem."

"Tell me"

"I don't believe any of this."

"Any of what?"

"This." Martin spread his arms wide and waved at the world in general, or what little world there was to see.

"What, the mist?"

"No, all of it. The train, the cottage, the party. You."

"I see," considered the old man. "That is a problem."

"A big one."

The old man thought for a moment. "In that case, may I ask where you think you are ?"

Martin shrugged. "For all I know I could be face down in a puddle somewhere, and this could all be one big alcoholic dream."

"It's pretty complex dream, I must say. Shows a creative mind."

"Believe me, there's great swathes of my brain that have not been doing much lately. I reckon they'd have enough energy to manage this."

"Still seems a little complicated to me."

"I agree, perhaps I need a CAT scan." The old man looked mildly offended. "O come on, Mel, what do you want me to believe? That I've been suddenly transported to my own personal Narnia, my own little magical world?"

"Do you know, there was a time not so long ago when Christmas itself was considered magical?"

"Yep, it was called childhood. I remember it well."

"Clearly, not well enough."

"Meaning?"

The old man sighed. "Have you thought of Christopher? He's still a child."

"O, don't start, please, I'm busy having a breakdown. Besides, I told you, my son hates Christmas as much as I do."

"I wouldn't be too sure about that, if I were you."

"Really? I think I know my son better than you, Mr Figment of My Imagination." Martin paused. When he spoke again, it was with a tiny element of doubt in his voice. "Anyway, he would have told me if he thought differently."

"Perhaps he loves you too much to say anything."

Martin looked to the foggy sky and shouted. "O, come on, give me a break. Surely it's time to wake up now."

"Why are you so resistant to the idea of something special happening, to there being something wonderful in the world?"

"You see, there you go again. It's not just you, Mel, it's the whole thing you're trying to sell."

"I'm not trying to *sell* anything, Martin."

"You know what I mean – Christmas, joy to the world and everything. I just don't buy it."

"Selling *and* buying; Christmas has come a long way in your world."

"If you know anything about me – and considering you probably only exist in my head, you must do – then you know Christmas was bought and sold years ago."

"Three years ago"

"Thank you for the reminder, subconscious."

There was silence for a few minutes. Despite his cynicism, Martin did not know what to think. He walked around in the mist, head down, his mind racing. The old man looked on, clearly concerned.

Suddenly Martin stopped. In a low voice liberally sprinkled with scepticism, he asked, "So, if I believe, will I get her back?"

"It doesn't work like that, Martin," replied the old man softly.

Somewhere deep inside Martin's disbelieving brain, the disappointment clawed at him.

He raised his head. "Well, how does it work, then?" he asked abruptly. "Stanley gets his dad back, his past and future changed, and all I get is a kind old madman who wants me to be more jolly once a year."

"I'm sorry to disappoint," said the old man sincerely.

There were a few seconds of quiet as Martin searched the lines of the old man's face, but then the moment passed.

"Don't worry. It's not your fault," he said, turning his gaze once more downwards. "I'm afraid it's just typical of me. I can't even think up a happy ending for my own delusion."

Martin kicked his heels on the damp cobbles, his mind beaten and elsewhere.

"I miss her so much," he said. "But I expect you know that."

The old man's voice seemed to flow effortlessly through the mist. It was deep and sodden with compassion. "Would it help if I told you that she is somewhere very special; that she is no longer in pain and she loves you both very much."

Martin turned to the old man, tears beginning to well. "How can I believe that, when I don't believe any of this? How can I believe in this great big Christmas thing you keep telling me about, when the only thing Christmas ever did for me was take away the wife I loved and the mother Christopher adored."

"I know it's hard, Martin, but Christmas is about more than a date, a day of the year."

"Prove it, then. Come on, if you don't just exist in my sad little brain, then you ought to be able to prove it. And don't hide behind that old free will and faith thing. Prove there's still some magic left in the world. Show me something genuinely wonderful to do with Christmas and I'll believe you."

The old man seemed hesitant and unsure. Even in his torment, Martin could see these were not feelings to which the old man was accustomed.

"You see, you can't, can you?"

"Martin ..."

"I know, I know, it doesn't work like that. No, of course it doesn't."

The old man looked upwards. The mist had begun to clear above them.

"I'd like you to leave now, please, Mel. Wherever you exist, in my head, in my dreams or in some weird fantasy world, I'm saying thanks, it's been nice knowing you, but I'd really would like you to leave."

Martin's sadness was complete and all-consuming, which was why he did not notice the fog dissolve around him and the cobbles fade in to a million grains of sand under his feet. He only looked up when he felt the warm desert wind on his face, and when he did, he was surprised to see the old man staring disbelievingly around him.

23.
SOMETHING WONDERFUL

The streets were crowded with people, despite the hour. A great, churning, eddying river of humanity poured through the small desert town. It spread out from the main gate and swirled noisily back and forth along the narrow lanes as streams of tired travellers ebbed and flowed between the mud-walled houses bartering for food and shelter. They were guided through the darkness by the oil lamps that hung from the more impressive dwellings, sweetening the air with the scent of olives. The lamps burned with a steady heat, but the light they cast was muted by the plumes of fine dust scuffed up by the hundreds of sandaled feet tramping across the bone-dry, sandy streets. Old men sat outside inns on rough wooden benches drinking wine and honeyed water, and looked on impassively at the commotion. Others struggled from door to door seeking lodgings, their spines, already brittle with time, bent further by the weight of the load they carried. Along the main street, big, bearded bedouins dressed in grimy robes pulled entire families on carts to the town's small square, where street vendors had set up impromptu stalls selling figs and dates and raisins. Some of the more adventurous were charcoaling chickens in the embers of fires hurriedly dug in the sand. The smoke from the fires hung in the still air and combined with the dust to form a thin, sandy smog which settled over the town, blocking out the stars and causing the youngest and oldest lungs to grate and splutter. On several corners, small groups of teenage boys gathered to eye up the new visitors and to wonder if their quiet little town would ever be so alive again.

Some people had bought donkeys from merchants in nearby villages. They were fine for transport outside, but fully ladened they struggled to cope with the busy and noisy darkness of the town's crowded little lanes. A couple of children, barefoot, bare-chested and buzzing at being out so late, took turns ducking beneath the legs of one of donkeys hemmed in by the horde. The animal eventually panicked and began to buck wildly, sending the contents of its sacks clattering on to the stone steps of one of the bigger houses of the town. Its frightened braying and flailing legs inevitably distressed the other donkeys nearby, one of which carried a heavily pregnant young woman, and it took all the strength of a watching innkeeper to calm the animal before her husband arrived to lift his tired and frightened wife to safety.

"You're not an easy person to get rid of, are you?" said Martin with an air of resignation. He wasn't sure if he should be annoyed or amused. "You're certainly the most tenacious hallucination I've ever had." Martin looked out at the desert town below them. "And inventive," he added.

They stood on the walls of the main gate to the town and gazed down at the crowds that poured through the central street.

"Still, somewhere warm. At least that makes a change."

The old man did not answer. Instead, he stared around him, his expression a mixture of joy and amazement. He then closed his eyes and inhaled deeply, as if savouring the smells of the scene below.

"Are you okay?" asked Martin. "Although, granted, that seems a strange thing for me to be asking you."

"I'm fine," the old man replied, his eyes still closed. "I'm absolutely fine." He then looked over at Martin and smiled mischievously, "But thanks for your concern."

"So, where are we now?" asked Martin.

"O, you'll like it here," he bubbled.

"Why?"

"They don't have Christmas."

"Promising," Martin acknowledged. "It's very busy. What's everyone doing?"

"They're just like you and me, Martin," he said, beaming widely. "They're going home."

"So, I *am* going home?" interrupted Martin. "I was beginning to think you'd kidnapped me."

"Kidnapped by your own subconscious?" remarked the old man. "I expect that would be quite difficult." His gaze fell upon something. "Come on, we need to get going," he suddenly announced and began to hurry down the mud steps.

Martin did not move.

"Come on, Martin, we need to go," beckoned the old man.

"Mel, I meant what I said before."

"I know."

"Then why have we come here?"

The old man walked back up the steps and looked at Martin with his kind, rheumy eyes. He placed both hands softly on his shoulders and in a deep, mellifluous voice, worn smooth with time, he said, "Because something wonderful is about to happen."

Martin was staggered. They were in the square and never before had he experienced such a combined and unnerving assault on his senses. For a start, it was very noisy. People were chattering and shouting and bargaining and selling, and all at such a volume it was difficult to pick out any specific conversation. To Martin's unfamiliar ears it merged in to one incessant, cackling call. It was also extremely crowded, with most of the travellers packed in to such a tiny space that movement became a matter of physically shoving your way forward. This had the combined effect of causing the crowd to sway en masse in one direction and then collectively and inescapably in the other, until like the tiny segments of a giant caterpillar, people were squeezed inexorably to the front, before being eventually ejected in to the freedom of the streets.

Martin could see little of his surroundings. The light from the fires and from the lamps which overhung the square provided him with brief glimpses, but in a night darkened further by smoke and dust, he could see nothing beyond the people momentarily squashed against him as he was pressed through the multitude. A parade of quick and slightly disquieting flashes passed swiftly before him of frightened, toothless women and of fine-boned, sun-blackened men; of laughing young boys, their faces painted with ochre, and pretty girls with dazzling smiles and brightly coloured headdresses; of greasy vendors carrying spits of chickens, and donkeys carrying a family's life. The smells also came thick and fast, from chicken fat to rose petal oil, from spices to asses, sweat to sand.

And all the time he was being jostled and bumped. His feet were being trodden on and his chest crushed. It was too much. He looked over at the old man for help, but he appeared to be enjoying every minute of it. Wedged in the middle of the crowd, jammed between a huge, black-robed man and his three excited children, he looked entirely at home and had a smile so wide it shone through his whiskers.

"Mel!" Martin shouted, but the old man did not hear. "Mel, can we get out of here?" he called, but again there was no response. Then Martin remembered where he was, and in a low, calm voice that was completely lost amongst the wailing crowd, he said, "Mel, help me."

Immediately the noise of the square seemed to dim and the old man looked over. Within seconds he was at Martin's side.

"Oops, sorry about that," he said. "Lost myself for a minute there."

"Can we get out of here, please?"

"Of course. I forgot it can be a little intimidating if you're not used to it." The old man dusted himself down, panting with pleasure. "Any preferences? After all, it's your dream."

"Somewhere I can breathe would be nice."

Several minutes later they had glided effortlessly through the throng and were walking along the main dusty street. Martin was relieved to be out of the madness of the square. If truth be told, the whole experience had left him a little shaken and edgy.

"How are you feeling?" asked the old man.

"I'm okay," he lied. "I could do with sitting down for a minute or two, though. Is that allowed?"

"I think we can make an exception. We've got some time to spare."

"Good. How about here?" asked Martin, pointing to a small inn.

The inn appeared to be the standard type of establishment for the town. It's low, mud and stone walls were reddish-brown, as if burnished by the sun, and stretched back from the main street to a small yard beyond. Its roof of thin reed and cloth hung limply across the diagonal cypress beams that topped the building and drooped over the flimsy awnings erected out the front. There were several wooden benches lined haphazardly outside, all of which were full of men drinking and laughing with only the occasional nod of interest to the travellers wandering up and down the main street. These were clearly menfolk who lived in the town. Inside, the scene was very different. It was only moderately busy, but everybody was a visitor and appeared to be carrying a burden of some sort, either a heavy bag or a young infant or simply the weariness of too much time spent walking in the sun. The owner and his helpers buzzed around trying to help the new arrivals – most wanted drink, some needed food and everyone seemed to be looking for somewhere to stay –

but his resources were meagre and running out fast. The town was clearly not built for so many visitors.

"I know we're invisible and all that, but is there any way we could get a drink?"

"I don't see why not," replied the old man, his face sunny with exertion.

They made their way over to one of less crowded tables in the corner and sat down opposite each other on the end of two rough-hewn cedar benches. Also sitting at the table were a young family whose two small children were clearly exhausted from the day's travails. The youngest child, a pretty, brown haired daughter in a long smock, was fast asleep in the basket which the mother had hoped to fill with bread. Next to the family sat an old woman by herself sipping from a small water skin. She was dressed in a black woollen robe and was stick-thin. She appeared unmoved by the fussing going on around her and gave the impression that she had seen it all before. At the end of the table were the young pregnant woman who had narrowly escaped injury on the donkey, and her tired looking husband. He was very attentive and appeared to be reassuring her, but she seemed to be still distressed by the incident. On the other side sat a middle-aged couple eating cheese and dried plums. He was portly, dressed in garishly coloured, striped robes and was thoroughly enjoying himself; she was a petite woman with delicate features who, as was obvious to everyone but her husband, just wanted to go to bed.

"Two beakers of wine, please," called the old man to the owner.

The innkeeper was a wiry man with a kind face, and despite being busy trying to sort out some food for a group of hungry travellers on another table, he quickly and adeptly poured two wooden beakers of wine from a jug on the bar. He then momentarily looked at the beakers with complete bewilderment, as if unaware of what he had just done.

"I'm a bit confused. Are we here or not?" asked Martin.

"We're definitely here, but we're only supposed to be visiting. Having a look."

"Can he see us then?"

"Erm, no, not really," replied the old man, a touch embarrassed. "I've just bent the rules a little bit. I thought a small drink was in order."

"Good decision," affirmed Martin.

The innkeeper finished his dealings with the other travellers, filled up a large tray with food and drink, including the two men's wines, and brought it over to the table.

"I've managed to find some more bread and a little meat," he said to the young family sitting next to Martin, and laid out a small bowl with two thin slices of dried mutton, a hunk of unleavened bread and some olives.

"Thank you very much," said the father, pulling out some coins from the small bag attached to his belt. He broke the bread in to smaller chunks and, together with his wife, began to feed his tired and hungry children.

The innkeeper turned his attention to the old lady and the pregnant woman and her husband. Martin looked on, impatient for his drink

"The last of the proper rooms have gone, I'm afraid," said the owner, placing on the table a voluminous jug of water sweetened with date syrup. "But I do have an old room out the back that you're all welcome to use. It's a bit messy, but it's warm and pretty clean."

The three visitors looked at each other.

"They'll be no charge," added the innkeeper.

The old lady had been watching the couple for the past half hour or so.

"You two take it," she said. "I suspect you need it more than me," she added kindly, looking at the exhausted woman. "Besides,

I'm quite enjoying myself here. An old woman like me doesn't often get time for such company and at such a late hour."

The couple hesitated for a moment out of basic politeness, but they had neither the energy nor the inclination to argue. The husband thanked the old lady effusively and helped his wife to her feet. She smiled sweetly at the old lady.

"Bless you," she said gratefully.

The innkeeper pointed to the side of the bar. "It's through that door and then round the back of the yard," he instructed. "I've put some mats and blankets in there, so it should be nice and cosy. There's a lamp, as well."

The couple shuffled off to the door.

The innkeeper looked at the two pots of wine left on his tray with a baffled expression. He scanned around the bar, as if looking for something. The puzzle clearly unresolved, he picked up the tray, walked to the old man and Martin and placed the two beakers in front of them without acknowledging their presence or, in fact, without appearing to be aware of what he was doing. Then, none the wiser, he rushed off back to the bar to deal with more requests for help.

"Still bending the rules a little?" suggested Martin, picking up his beaker.

The old man smiled.

"I'm sure I'll be forgiven. It's been a long night." He arched his eyebrows and added, "With a few surprises." He tapped his pot against Martin's. "I thought a little celebration was in order."

"What are we celebrating?"

"Going home."

Martin half-nodded. "Perhaps that's best left until I get there."

"You can go whenever you like."

"But I thought we were going to witness 'something wonderful'."

"You have."

"What do you mean?"

"Just then."

Martin shrugged.

"Don't you think the innkeeper was being kind just then?"

Martin stared blankly at the old man. "Sorry, I don't understand."

"The owner."

"He gave the kids some food, yes, ..."

The old man smiled encouragingly.

"... and let the other couple stay round the back ..." Martin paused. "... for nothing."

The old man nodded. "He did. Wonderful, wasn't it?"

"I'm assuming you're joking."

"No."

Martin's brow wrinkled in confusion.

"Mel, please tell me you're not being serious."

The old man simply stared at Martin, a grin playing at the edges of his mouth.

"You're not telling me that's it?"

The old man raised his eyebrows and smiled.

"That's it?!" Martin said incredulously. "That's the special moment you've dragged me here for?"

"Ah-ha."

"The offer of free bed and board, that's the magic that's going to make me believe?!"

"Yes," the old man bellowed.

"Now I know I'm dreaming." Martin turned away from the old man. "It might be you who needs help, Mel," he huffed.

Martin sat for a few moments grumbling to himself. The old man remained quiet as Martin drummed his fingers noisily on the table, the frustration building with every tap.

"Do you know, you nearly had me for a while," he said finally, unable to look the old man in the eyes. "You did, you know. You nearly had me thinking that, perhaps, just perhaps, there was something more out there, something better."

The old man's deep, soft voice floated across the noisy bar, heavy with meaning. "Martin, from that one act of kindness, all other acts of kindness will follow."

"And what's that supposed to mean?"

The old man leaned across the table. "That simple act of compassion is the seed from which will grow every other act of compassion at Christmas and beyond. Every charitable deed, every selfless gift. And grow it will, spreading through humanity like the sweetest vine, fruiting on the natural goodness in people's hearts. It will feed every Christmas tree, shine on every star, illuminate every child's smile. Wonderful, simply wonderful."

Martin was puzzled. "Sorry, Mel, I thought you said they didn't have Christmas here."

"They don't. Not yet."

There was a pause.

"Where are we, Mel?" Martin asked hesitantly.

"Bethlehem."

The bedlam of the inn seemed to dampen and recede, as Martin battled to make sense of the old man's words. This could not be right. On so many levels, this could not be right.

"No," managed Martin, shaking his head. "No, you're not getting me with this."

The old man's face remained expressionless.

"You can't ask me to accept this," Martin grimaced, the ramifications of the old man's assertions too monumental to consider. "You mean ...?" the question tailed off.

The old man nodded.

Martin rubbed his head with his hands. "Okay, I want to wake up now." He looked upwards and shouted. "Do you hear me? I want to wake up now."

The old man reached forward and placed his large hands on Martin's clenched fists.

"Come with me, Martin. Come with me and let's go and see."

Martin pulled away. "Absolutely not. This is way beyond what I expected. Way beyond."

"I give you my word," soothed the old man's voice, "there is nothing to be frightened of."

After several seconds, Martin relaxed his grip on the table.

"You've come so far," encouraged the old man.

"You're right, I have." His voice was quivering. "And this is far enough, thank you."

"It seems a pity not to finish your journey."

Without warning, the innkeeper suddenly arrived at their table and began to wash down the wooden surface with a frayed piece of sheepskin. Although clearly oblivious of the two men, he was somehow aware of the space they occupied and he manoeuvred himself around the old man and Martin with balletic ease. Both men's eyes were drawn to the acrobatic display.

Martin shook his head and broke in to a reluctant smile. "Don't you ever give up?" he groaned.

"What sort of guide would I be if I did?" replied the old man.

"Mel, I'm – I'm just a normal man. I'm nothing special. Just a normal bloke with a young son."

"And that's why I cannot think of a better person to be here with," he reassured, taking Martin by the arm.

After a few seconds of token resistance, Martin finished his drink and allowed himself to be led round the back of the inn, fighting the panic of his convictions with every step.

*

The yard was moderately big and contained the usual detritus of a first century inn. Battered wooden crates filled mostly with wind-blown sand stood in one corner, together with a pile of broken jugs and pots, the clay shards of which were spread all over the dirt-floor. Standing against the back of the inn and sheltered from the sun were huge stone urns used for storing dried figs, dates, olives and other fruit. They were all empty now, except for the smallest urn; the innkeeper's wife always kept this full for when times were lean. A line of washing, propped up by the broken arm of a small plough, hung across the yard, the robes and smocks dangling limply in the still night. A small well had recently been dug in the corner and next to it, piled inside each other, were three new wooden pails. The stones around the well were darkened with damp and the moist sand contained the busy tracks of mice and rats.

One side of the yard was made up of a small pen. On the thick, fresh-smelling hay slept a donkey and two oxen. The animals stirred and snorted with the approach of the two men. Just off the pen was a side room. Through the open window Martin could the see shadows of the pregnant woman and her husband silhouetted in the lamp hanging from the thick beam.

"That's it, that's enough," said Martin fearfully. "I don't need to go any further."

"What are you afraid of?"

"I don't know." Martin began to pace around the yard, his mind beating at the door of his beliefs. "I – I don't know."

The pacing quickened, his mind painfully alive with conflicting emotions.

"I must have invented this, mustn't I?" he mumbled to himself. "Conjured it up in my addled and unemployed brain?" He continued stomping around the yard. "It's the only answer," he confirmed. "Nothing else makes sense."

The old man looked on with concern, but kept silent.

Martin was breathing heavily now, his brow shiny with perspiration. "But how could I have made this up?" he asked the night. "I don't know enough about it. I mean, you know, I never was particularly attentive at school."

The old man went to say something, but Martin was there first.

"No, nothing from you," he interjected. "You've freaked me out enough as it is."

In the quiet of the yard, the sounds of Martin's thumping mingled with the grunting of the sleeping donkey and the occasional hushed voices of the expectant couple.

Martin stopped walking and looked straight at the old man, yearning for an explanation. "But, I don't believe, Mel. You know, I don't believe."

The old man hesitated. "Do you think you're imagining this?" he gently prompted.

"I'm not sure," replied Martin immediately. He then added, "How can I be? We both know I'm not good enough to think up an entire world I never knew existed."

"If you're not imagining it, well, you must be here. That must really be sand on your shoes; you must really have a beaker in your hand. And if you believe you're here, then, Martin, you believe."

Martin said nothing for a few moments.

"Not good enough, Mel, I'm afraid. This is too much to be explained away by some fancy words."

"What would you have me say?"

"I don't know. I need something more. Something just a bit more."

The old man nodded understandingly. For a few seconds all was quiet. The oxen shuffled on their straw, water dripped in to the well. Then the still of the night was disturbed by the gentle flapping of the clothes on the washing line as the warm desert wind began to blow from the East. No more than a light breeze at first, it soon gathered strength, and as it did so it gradually blew away the dust and smoke that hung over the town and revealed the staggering sweep of the heavens above. And Martin finally saw it. The Star shone down on the yard with a startling light, glowing with the brilliance of every candle ever lit for Christmas, and burned away his disbelief.

He was asleep before he hit the ground.

24.
HANSON GREEN

The train pulled slowly in to the small suburban station. It was the last train home for Christmas and was only five minutes late. Given the weather, the driver considered this to be something of an achievement.

Hanson Green was two stops before the line ended in rural anonymity in a small market town in West Sussex, and the station's guard had left for a real fire and a pint of warm ale with his friends several hours before. No-one would notice, he had reasoned; it was not the busiest line, especially this far out. He was right. There were only two passengers left on the train.

The old man leaned over and gently shook the sleeping Martin.

"Martin, we're here. It's your stop."

Martin stirred slowly. He had been asleep since the desert and it took a while for the experiences of the past few hours to arrange themselves in to a cognitive thought. The fact that he was clearly not in the last place he remembered was, by now, something to be expected.

"If I ask you where we are, will I regret it?" he ventured.

"I'm not sure."

"Where are we?"

"We're just pulling in to Hanson Green," replied the old man matter-of-factly. "On a train."

"Oh," Martin allowed. He looked around at the tediously familiar train carriage and glanced at his watch. It read half past ten.

"Time moves on, eh?"

"It does."

Martin exhaled noisily. He stretched out his arms and turned his neck side to side. It was stiff from his sleeping and made several loud clicks.

"Mine does that," offered the old man.

They met each other's gaze and started to laugh.

As the laughter petered out, Martin asked, "Mel, just for a minute I'm going to pretend that you're a normal person. I'm going to ask you a question and I'd like to know if you wouldn't mind giving me a straight answer? One without any meaningful pauses or knowing looks?"

"I'll try."

"Ok. Here goes. Have I been, where I think I've been?"

"It depends on where you think you've been, I suppose."

"Arrgh! Just for once ... Look, was it all true?"

"It really isn't ..."

"Straight answer, Mel. Was it all true?"

There was a touching quality of irreverence about Martin, and the old man looked at him with great fondness.

"Yes," he confirmed.

Martin closed his eyes and let the relief swell within him. He sighed as he felt the meaning start to come back in to his life, seeping in to hollows that had echoed with nothing but grief for the past three years. Hope, he decided, was a wonderful thing.

He opened his eyes and looked out at the station through the grimy window. The yellow lights of the platform shone feebly on his face.

"And those things you told me about my wife, are they true?" he calmly asked, his gaze fixed firmly outside the train. "You know, that she's somewhere special and she loves us?"

"Yes."

"Does she worry about us?"

"Every day."

"Tell her." He began to choke, but quickly recovered. "Tell her, I miss her, but that everything is going to better from now on. Can you do that? For me? For Christmas?"

"Martin, my friend. It is already done."

Martin turned to look at the old man, his eyes wet with unspoken words.

After a few moments, he turned back to the window.

"I - I suppose I better get off. Don't want to miss my stop," he sniffed.

"The train will not leave until you are ready. But time is now running and you have a home and a son to go to."

Martin wiped his eyes and stood to leave.

"How much will I remember?"

"You'll remember all you need to."

"Will that be much?"

"I suspect it will be more than you think."

"More than a dream?"

"Much more."

"Good. I haven't dreamt in a while."

"Perhaps now you will."

"That would be nice."

Martin opened the train door.

"Thanks, Mel. It doesn't seem enough, but thanks."

"It's more than enough, Martin. More than enough."

Martin stepped on to the platform and watched as the train pulled away in to the darkness. He did not move until its lights had faded completely in to the night. And then he turned to make his way home.

It was snowing. The wind had eased, the temperature had dropped a critical few degrees and it was snowing more heavily than anyone had seen in years. Thick, downy flakes floated soundlessly to the ground and cushioned Martin's footsteps as he wandered home through the light and silence of Hanson Green.

He had worn a broad smile all the way from the station, grinning at the spectacular Christmas card the village had become and wondering whether this was also the old man's doing. He rather fancied Mel was a man for the final flourishing cliché.

His street was barely recognizable from the one he'd left that morning. A deep layer of snow carpeted every house and garden, softening the light from the street lamps and hushing all but the most raucous of celebrations. Such peaceful surroundings found an echo in Martin's heart which would have been unthinkable barely hours before. As if on cue, from across the green came the muffled sounds of the church choir warming up for Midnight Mass; wonderfully joyful, tremendously uplifting and every chord indelibly marked with the old man's hand. Even if he was supposed to forget, he knew he would remember this.

Martin turned in to his drive and looked up to see the light still on in Christopher's bedroom. He was pleased, if a little anxious. The little lad had deserved more of his dad over the last three years and the guilt he felt was the only thing that weighed down on the new lightness of his being. The first thing they would do tomorrow is get a tree.

He quietly let himself in and crept up the stairs. It would be nice to surprise him. Bursting in to Christopher's bedroom, smile at the ready, he was surprised to find an empty bed. Strange, he thought. Martin then went to his own bedroom to see if Christopher had fallen asleep in there; certainly not that unusual for this night of all nights. But that was empty as well.

He was just beginning to get anxious when he noticed the attic door was ajar. Trying not to make any noise, he picked up the old broom handle they kept by the bathroom door, quietly pulled down the small loft ladder and climbed up in to the attic.

A new light had been installed a few months ago and Martin reached out to switch it on before realising it was unnecessary. At one end of the attic was the normal collection of boxes, old furniture, bric-a-brac and assorted jetsam of a small suburban family. One of the boxes had been recently opened and was lying on its side. By the dim light of the old, bare sixty watt bulb that hung from the joist Martin could just make out the words "Xmas Decorations" in Mary's handwriting.

At the other end lay Christopher, fast asleep and wrapped in a duvet. Next to him was a small artificial Christmas tree, enthusiastically decorated with some tattered silver tinsel and two somewhat incongruous, expandable paper lanterns. Underneath the tree was a little box of Turkish delight, Martin's favourite. The box had been prised open and one of the sweets removed, Martin noted. On top of the box, in rough, immature writing, scored in to the lid through the covering cellophane, were the words: "Happy Birthday Daddy". Next to this, propped up against a model of a beaming and all-too-familiar Father Christmas, his white beard and fur-trimmed coat twinkling with glitter, was a large framed photo. Martin picked it up. It was the one taken of the three of them at the Christmas grotto where they had taken Christopher when he was just an infant. They were all laughing inexplicably at the photographer. Martin had not seen it in years.

"Daddy," mumbled Christopher, waking slowly from his slumber. "I'm glad your home."

Martin leaned down and kissed him on the cheek.

"So am I," he whispered.

EPILOGUE:
THE END

The train driver clambered out of the cab, pulled his coat around him and tramped out in to the snow to meet his wife who was waiting in the station's car park. It had taken a little longer than normal to complete the manifest, but he was pleased to be finally on his way. The small hatchback chugged throatily out of the car park, its windscreen wipers swishing maniacally back and forth, and turned down the hill for a short and at times hair-raising journey back to the couple's little cottage. Very soon the growling of the engine faded in to the night and the station was left in silence.

For a while nothing happened. Eventually the station's time switch flipped to midnight and one by one the brash fluorescent lights clicked off, and the whole station flickered in to darkness.

The snow continued to fall, piling high on the roof of the train, muting the sounds of the night. An owl hooted, a bell pealed, a door slammed, all seemingly miles away, dampened in to the distance by the deep wintry blanket that cushioned the world.

The old man sat on the carriage brimming with contentment. He loved these moments. Alone, after the evening's adventures, just him and the wonder of the Day. It had been a tiring night and he wrapped his thick, fur-lined coat around him and sank in to the beauty of it all.

The soft, ethereal light of the snow illuminated his white beard and wistful smile as he reflected on the evening. It had been difficult one, he decided, but fulfilling nonetheless. All of them had eventually taken their favoured path, which was unusual, although in Martin's case, it had been a close-run thing. The old man wasn't surprised. Grief can do that to a person. Christopher should see him through now.

After several minutes there was the soft sound of footsteps shuffling along the platform. The old man listened as they padded slowly through the thick snow until they stopped directly outside his carriage.

The compartment door opened. "Good evening, old friend," said Caspar, clambering inside. He brushed the snow from his greatcoat and removed his hat. "I trust it has been a *good* evening?"

"A very good evening," replied the old man. "How about you?"

"As exhausting as ever, but mostly successful, which is what counts." He sat down opposite the old man and roared with relief. "Oo, that's better."

"Anywhere interesting?" asked Balthazar, climbing in behind Caspar.

"Well, yes." The old man paused, dragging out the moment, a hint of mischief in his voice. "I've been home."

"Home?" boomed Balthazar. "You've been home?!" He was a large man with a bushy beard and eyebrows, and his eyes twinkled at the news. "Oh, this I have to hear. You always were the favoured one, Melchior."

The three men laughed.

"Right, tell us all about it, and don't leave out a single thing," insisted Caspar, now thoroughly revived.

Melchior did not let them down. He told them of the desert, and of the square, and of the Star, and as the three old friends once again revelled in each other's company, the train pulled away, leaving just the snow falling silently on to an empty track.

ABOUT THE AUTHOR

Tony Wilson was born in 1960 and grew up in Bermondsey, London. He spent his earliest Christmases in a cavalry suit playing Scalextric with his brother, Gary, who was dressed as a Roman. This still affects him deeply. He is a practising physiotherapist who has written many academic papers, but this is his first foray in to fiction. He lives on the South Coast, near Chichester, with his partner Lucy and three children, JJ, Amy and Holly.

Printed in Great Britain
by Amazon.co.uk, Ltd.,
Marston Gate.